I0725680

**Felix Publishing 2020**
email: info.felixpublishing@gmail.com
Print copies available from publisher.

**Tom Shipley's War: Memoirs of a Weekend Warrior**

2020 digital book release
ISBN: 978-1-925662-35-1
Print Edition
ISBN: 978-1-925662-34-4
Author: Dr. Peter T. Scott

Registration:
Thorpe-Bowker +61 3 8517 8342
email: bowkerlink@thorpe.com.au
No part of this publication may be reproduced, stored in a retrieval system, or transmitted in any form or by any means, electronic, mechanical, photocopying, recording or otherwise, without the prior written permission of the publisher.

# Tom Shipley's War:
## Memoirs of a
## Weekend Warrior

## Peter T. Scott

First released 2020

To the former members of the Citizen's Military Forces
and the current members of Army Reserve.

This book is a work of fiction. Any resemblance to people living or dead is purely coincidental. Some characters may be a blend of several personalities and multiple locations over many years. Some incidents as described in this book did happen.

# Contents

# Chapter One: All the Way with LBJ

In one respect, 1965 was not a good year. Excited by starting my teaching career at the beginning of the year, it was also a time when the war in Vietnam was getting very hot. The government had decided to 'go all the way with LBJ'[1] and commit more of the country's Armed Forces to the war. Unfortunately, more men than were readily available were needed so compulsory conscription was introduced the previous year for all males turning twenty years of age. I would be twenty in the September of 1965 Damn!

Conscription was very unpopular in Australia, although the country had been in most wars since its inception in 1901. I guess that we are a belligerent lot! This time around, a ballot system of birthdates suggested some sort of equality and fairness in the system but most people had their doubts. Although a nation of gamblers, this was one lottery that no-one wanted, except the politicians who had allowed the country to be dragged into yet another foreign

---

[1] Lyndon Baines Johnson (1908 – 1973), often referred to by his initials LBJ, was the 36th president of the United States from 1963 to 1969.

conflict. Conscription had been introduced in mid-1942, during the Second World War when the country was under threat from invasion. Under this scheme all men aged eighteen and over were required to join the Citizens Military Forces (CMF). Volunteers who joined the regular army, the Australian Imperial Force (AIF) scorned these CMF conscripts as chocolate soldiers, or chockos, because they were believed to melt under the conditions of battle. Things were little different in 1965 except that now one had one's name in the barrel for the luck of the draw in the ballot.

There were some limited alternatives, apart from declaring one's insanity or committing a crime. Young boys of nineteen[2] who were students or those who could prove that they were conscientious objectors to all wars in general could apply to the courts for deferment but the government was very strict in these matters and it was probably easier to claim madness. Unfortunately, as it was considered crazy to go to war anyway, who could tell? The novel Catch 22 had been out a few years so the government were wary of such tactics and

---

[2] One was still considered legally as a 'child' if one was below the age of 21 at that time.

conscientious objectors in a belligerent society did not go down very well anyway. One of my old school friends had made such an appeal and earned himself a short time in prison for his beliefs. This did not seem an easy way out of the ballot.

Another way out for nineteen-year-olds was to get in quick and volunteer for the CMF. A few did but found that they had to be very efficient part-time soldiers for the equivalent of thirty-three days in each year. Failure to do so meant instant conscription regardless of one's birthdate with the distinct possibility of an all-expenses paid trip to Vietnam.

'All the way with LBJ' had been the American Democrat Party's campaign slogan in the 1964 elections and this soon became a buzzword for the war. The Australian Prime Minister also used this slogan to show his solidarity with the American policy in Vietnam. To some people, this must have been confusing when it was reported with great fanfare in the daily press – the main and often the only source of truth in the country. Well, almost! The same press also often referred to politicians of one party 'jumping into bed' with members of the opposition party and so this new expression of affection for American politics only confused the general public even more. But I didn't want to go there!

Personally, I had too many of my own concerns in 1965 and besides, I was not going to be twenty until September and that was a long way off. I was in my first school and matters of personal survival concerned the home front rather than a foreign war. It did occasionally occur to me during the rare fit of contemplation that there may be a problem in the future.

Many of my school friends who were slightly older than I, had suddenly received the dreaded 'call-up' notice in the first draft of the year. Most went willingly. After all, it was their duty to heed the call to arms from their country. It was the patriotic thing to do and there was initially a certain amount of adventure attached to it. One of my friends had been over-excited at this prospect and had purchased a T-shirt from some dubious military shop which read:

'JOIN THE ARMY. TRAVEL TO NEW COUNTRIES. MEET NEW PEOPLE, and then in very fine print it continued:

This was a rather sick comment as the sense of adventure for these young National Servicemen soon wore off after the tough training and the horrors of war.

There was also the belief at the time that perhaps our country was in real danger if the war in Vietnam was not successful. The infamous Domino Theory had been around since the 1950's and had been an excuse for intervention in Asia during most of the Cold War period. It was often quoted in the freedom-loving press, that now that China had fallen to the Communists, so too would the rest of Southeast Asia, including Thailand then Malaysia, then Indonesia and so on. Being the 'and so on' was not a popular idea at the time, so many thought that going to this war was a good thing. That didn't last!

Friday nights had always been one of socialising after school. Teachers would hit the lounge bar of the 'Statesman's Rest' hotel about four o'clock and have time to get in a few drinks before the rest of the drinking community arrived a little after five. About seven, it would occur to my friends and I that it was time that we should wander back to the hostel in which we lived to, 'fuel up' and so get ready for the later session of socialising later that night. This took the usual ritual of wandering in some form of a semicircular route back to the uninviting doors of our usual confinement, negotiating the few steps up onto the hostel's wooden veranda and then checking our mail boxes before suffering the necessary indignity of dining on what the cooks called 'food'.

It so happened that on one Friday evening, the automatic response of reaching into what would normally be an empty mail box, was rewarded with the presence of a long, brown envelope containing the federal government's well-known crest. Still endowed with the optimism fuelled by the usual Friday afternoon session and in great need of something more solid in my stomach, I stuffed the envelope into my coat pocket and weaved my way into the dining room after my friends.

Perhaps it was the enthusiasm of socialising earlier that afternoon, the quality of the food which had just been consumed or even the fact that I had had a tiring school week but now felt incredibly tired. To the derision of my colleagues at the dining table, I made my feeble excuses and wandered off to the solitude of my small room.

"Piker!" yelled Jacko.

"Yeah! And that too!" said Will, both of whom were not teachers and had started socialising at least an hour before me.

Managing, with some difficulty, to locate the bathroom, I then had to find which one of the many doors along the corridor with its faded, floral linoleum was in fact mine. Reaching room number E10, my designated cell, and having the usual multiple attempts at inserting my key into the microscopic keyhole, I managed to get into my room. Here, I took off my coat and put in temporarily on the back of my chair before it fell onto the floor, and fell into bed. The official-looking envelope and its contents would also have to wait in its coat pocket on the floor.

## Chapter Two: He Doth Protest Too Much!

The morning came with its usual glare of intense sunlight and the thumping people eagerly running down the corridor for another sumptuous lunch in our seedy hostel. There was something else trying desperately to force its way through the fog of my morning hangover. What was it!

The letter! I leaned out of my warm bed trying not to give up the contents of my stomach and searched the floor for my discarded coat. Perhaps I would also find my head there as well!

Feverishly fossicking, I found the inside coat pocket and its official government contents. With little ceremony and total indifference to the large government coat-of-arms on its surface, I ripped the envelope open and unfolded the neat, public-servant-folded letter with trembling fingers.

"You have been indefinitely deferred." It finally read after the obligatory few paragraphs about the threat to the country and the need for conscription. I guessed that the phrase 'indefinitely deferred' meant that my number did not come up in the ballot and that the luck of the draw meant that I had lost yet another lottery. Hurray for this one!

That made my day and I quickly sobered up, put my clothes back to some sort of shabby order and joined the other thumpers down the corridor to lunch.

"Good on ya, Hairy Legs!" said Jacko at the table.

"Does this mean that you are not going?" enquired Will who was often the last one in the bank to see the penny drop.

"Too right, Dog's Breath!" Jacko glared at Will. Jacko still had not fully recovered from the previous night.

Lunch was a poor substitute for the usually dismal breakfast on that Saturday morning. But the usual 'cold meat salad' seemed to be tastier this morning. Whether it was my need for food or the good news provided by the government was open to question but the day had certainly improved. Now I could get on with my life without having to join all of the other pre-twenty-year-old's worrying about the draft and their future.

"There's a ruckus going on at Civic this afternoon. Ya comin', Hairy Legs?" Jacko interrupted my happy thoughts.

By this he meant that there was an anti-Vietnam War protest scheduled for that afternoon in the main square of the city. Ever since it was announced that the country would 'go all the way' last year, there had been vocal misgivings about sending troops overseas to fight yet another war which the Americans had got into. The popular press, or so they liked to be called, opposed and supported this war depending upon pleas from concerned mothers or current trends in government expediency and calls from ex-soldier associations to support 'truth, justice and democracy'…whatever that really meant!

And so, the three amigos wandered up to the centre of the city where the main highway crossed one of the many large circular roads which formed the city's cobweb road pattern. Quite a crowd had gathered there and it was becoming a regular weekend habit and source of entertainment for the indifferent of the populace.

There were four corners at this major intersection – a redundant observation under usual circumstances but here and now there were four distinctly separate street corners.

On one of the corners, making most of the noise and creating more overlap onto the street and showing little respect for those few midday shoppers, were the anti-war protestors. Most were in their 'rent-a-crowd uniform of torn blue (once) jeans, slogan-bearing T-shirt, sandals (if formally attired) and long hair. Males could be distinguished from females only because of size (often doubtful) and the cut of their jeans. At college biology classes, I had learnt the valuable lesson that males could always be distinguished from females because of their genes but it was not obvious in all cases on the street.

This feral group made a lot of noise with their whistles and home-made drums. They had badly-scrawled placards expressing their contempt in the minimal number of words such as 'OUT NOW!' NO WAR! 'F**K LBJ' and so on. Most had pretensions of being students but were generally unemployed except for those few who were, and who also had exemptions from National Service. This was in keeping with such protests of social disorder, whether they be anti-war, anti-conscription, anti-pollution, anti-government or anti-work. Such groups had been around for centuries and usually consisted of younger people who did not seem to fit into society and wanted to make themselves known. There were also some better-dressed people who genuinely disagreed with the latest entry into international warfare and wanted to express themselves in a coherent and justified manner. Not a hope!

Diagonally and diametrically opposed to this group was the other rowdy bunch of protesters. Unlike their feral opponents across the street, these protestors were clean-cut, had short hair and wore their characteristic uniform of corduroy trousers and jacket, clean shirts and ties and highly polished shoes. These were the gentlemen of the local Military Academy and their placards were more carefully written in army post-modernist stencils. 'SUPPORT OUR BOYS IN VIETNAM', 'SAVE DEMOCRACY' and other nationalistic slogans were on their banners. They were generally quieter than the feral group except for the occasional personal jeer or four-letter anatomical word in reply to some coarse remark personally made in their direction by one or more of the ferals on the corner diagonally opposite. They did, however, have a collective manner that suggested that they would happily go across the street and bring peace to their opponents in the most violent of ways.

Their inability to do so was ensured by the large contingent of uniformed police on the third street corner. They had also been joined by members of the general public who had casually wandered over to see what all of the fuss was about. The protection offered on this corner made it the obvious place of security for onlookers. It was to this group that the three amigos sauntered.

The fourth street corner was probably the largest and quietest group of all four congregations. This corner was occupied by the Press. In a variety of normal, civilian attire, these men, and a few women, where easily identified by their cameras and notepads. Occasionally one would suddenly decamp for the nearest telephone, having thought of a great headline or story line for their editor. Regardless of the actual individual dramas being played on the other corners, the headlines that evening in the newspapers would be in keeping with the need for their editors to keep their owners happy and their desire to sell newspapers or advertising space on television.

The more conservative of the national newspapers, being printed late that evening in a distant state capital, would probably have a more subdued heading on about page seven stating that there had been massed protests in the nation's capital that morning attended my hundreds of protesters. This number would, of course include all attendees including the gentlemen from the Military Academy, the Police and general public, their own colleagues and of course the smaller number of ferals with their forlorn number of genuine concerned anti-war protesters. Meanwhile the local tabloid would have a large front-page headline denouncing the war in general with a large photo of the more exotically-endowed female protester holding her placard in a most provocative manner. The local university student news rag would have an equally-large headline of 'POLICE BRUTALITY' based on the obscure fact that one of the Sergeants had requested the ferals to keep off the road and stop obstructing Saturday morning traffic. Well, there has always been freedom of the press in our country!

Now, don't get me wrong! I have nothing against protesting. As a young student teacher, I had been a student member of the Amalgamated Teachers'

Union and had joined the ranks of teachers outside of Parliament House in Sydney to protest the Education Department's reforms in introducing White Boards into the classroom. Our little protest was a relatively quiet and professional affair. Teachers generally had short hair, wore shoes and suits or at least shirts and ties and the ladies wore dresses down to the knees…as long as they were not of a red colour which the Department feared would inflame the passions of immoral males within the teacher ranks. We did not beat drums and carried few signs except a large banner which read SAVE OUR CHALK!

Back in the feral corner, whose number included a few acquaintances from my hostel, the chanting had become louder and the waving of signs became more threatening as more police had arrived. Diagonally across the intersection, the gentlemen of the Military Academy also had become more hostile and were now concentrating their protests directly against their opposition.

The Press contingent were also getting agitated as each group jockeyed for frontline position to take their photographs and take their notes.

Occasionally, someone would attempt to break through this scrum and dash to the nearest telephone to ring in another blow-by-blow description of what was happening. The whole matter became complicated when an Outside Broadcast television van from one of the local channels decided to park on their side of the intersection blocking most of the view.

To the quiet group of spectators, including Jacko, Will and myself on the other corner, the whole proceedings were of considerable entertainment value. Jacko would forget to which group he belong and would also yell some insult at the police who were no friends of his, having picked him up one night whilst speeding on his bicycle.

"On yer bike, Dog's breath!" he yelled at a motor cycle police officer across the street. Up until now, the police contingent had been called every four-letter word insult which the ferals could think of as well as a few longer words which conveyed similar meanings but nothing over two syllables as this went beyond their vocabulary. Dogs Breath sitting quietly on his motor cycle took exception to being told to get on his bike, which he was anyway, and motioned to two colleagues and pointed in our general direction. Unfortunately, Jacko as a surveyor's assistant for the National Survey Organisation, a quasi-autonomous non-governmental organisation, a government QUANGO, had no requirements to wear the standard public service uniform of shirt, tie, shoes and short hair. He, like many of the better class of ferals across the street wore faded jeans, long duffle coat and had long, straggly hair and a bushy black beard. He stood out in our little crowd of spectators. Seeing that he had become the target of potential police scrutiny, he turned and took off through the crowd. Will and I did likewise.

It was not the appearance of the ferals, nor their loud, unpleasant chanting which had put me off by their spectacle. To their way of thinking this was the only way to draw attention to the unfairness of the new conscription and of the new war in Asia. I agreed with their basic viewpoints but disagreed with their method. Within their ranks were some people who genuinely cared about the message which they were trying to get out to the general public; a body of people they arrogantly assumed knew nothing, said nothing and generally did even less. Unfortunately, their message was not coming through. Thanks to the large rent-a-crowd majority of loud protesters, the message somehow got lost. All the general public saw was a group of untidy and loud look-a-like individuals who disrupted the streets on what was supposed to be yet another cemetery-like quiet weekend in the nation's capital. The press added to their perception with the local tabloid's description of the ragged appearance and manners of these disrupters of society with little or no reference to the message of the protest. Consequently, the general public knew nothing more, said nothing and did even less.

So, time went on in that year of 1965. The cold classrooms of winter gave way to the artificial colours of spring and then the red brown dust of summer. By the beginning of the next year, the war in Vietnam had produced its first casualties of the new National Service men who had been drafted in the previous year. Brief letters from my childhood friend told of the uncertainty and fear of driving Army transports around Saigon, expecting a hand grenade from the hand of some innocent-looking street seller or child to be thrown into his cabin. The war was not going well and conscription had continued. The newspapers and nightly television were full of the horrors of this war; mainly the pitiful effects that it was having on the civilian population of Vietnam. Graphic images of villages which had been napalmed accidently by air strikes, were now hitting the headlines. Woman and children fleeing the destruction of their homes with allied troops standing in the background, seemingly indifferent to their plight.

By now the protest movement had also changed their tack. They had not gained much attention with their attempts to stop the war nor the process of conscription by their loud noise and antiwar placards. Now their attention was unfairly turned upon the very victims of one of their objections; the poor National Servicemen who had been conscripted and who went to serve their country right or wrong.

'BABY KILLERS!' 'DOWN WITH THE NACHOES' and other such misspelled and derogatory placards now harangued the ferals who had directed their hatred against the twice-yearly call-up victims. To the ferals, it was the National Servicemen who caused all of the atrocities of this war, not the politicians who had started it. This tenuous argument was supported in part by the tabloid press who found that they sold more newspapers and advertising space by reporting on the very real and unpleasant side of the war in Vietnam rather than the plight of the young men who were sent into it. The general public now knew a little about the war, as it received considerable nightly dramatic coverage on television, including much graphic footage with the usual pre-warning of "some viewers may not wish to watch the following scenes as they contain graphic images (but we are going to show them anyway!)" The general public still said very little except for those who joined the protest movement. Eventually the National Servicemen were treated badly for their involuntary call to fight for their nation. This made me mad!

How could I make my own protest of this injustice towards young men of my age, including some of my friends, who were now targeted as war criminals? I was a teacher and so a pillar of the very society causing this injustice. Any public activity on my part would result in instant dismissal from the teaching service. Perhaps I could write antagonistic anti-protest letters to the editors of the press under an assumed name? No. They would be edited out by the editors who wished to keep the conservative owners happy so that more newspapers and television advertising could be sold. Perhaps I could quietly indoctrinate my students about the respect for the country and duty which the conscriptees demonstrated against a sea of public antagonism? No. This would have been totally immoral and unprofessional in bringing politics into the classroom and besides, the oldest boys in the class were going to face the ballot of conscription in a few years themselves. Being a teenager in high school gave them enough anxiety and this reminder of a bleak future would not be right.

It so happens that I decided to do something very personal and extreme. I would volunteer for the local Citizens' Military Forces, or CMF, and put on army uniform to show these ferals that another part of the community supported the poor conscripts.

# Chapter Three: How Green was My Uniform?

The rowdy gang at our dining room table in the government hostel where I lived, consisted of the in-your-face and irrepressible Jacko, Will his more respected public servant friend and a few others who occasionally added to the irreverence of our nightly contempt of the hostel's food and general management. One of these was Jean Claude who worked in an obscure section of the government's Department of Administrative Administration. He did not say very much but usually agreed with the comments of those around our subversive table with a dopey smile, half closed eyes and a Gallic shrug of his shoulders. Jean Claude was not his real name of course. Nor was he French. His real name was Phineas Bottomly and he had come from Narrarooty, a small town in the southern state of Victoria. He used his pseudonym as his preferred name for obvious reasons to get over his mother's choice of names based on a Jules Verne character from the novel Around the World in Eighty Days which she had found one bleak morning during her pregnancy in the bleak town of Narrarooty. Phineas – sorry, Jean Claude, who was usually called J.C. by his friends – though more of connotations derived from a popular kick-boxer of movie fame. Besides he claimed that it pulled in the birds at parties. There were no ornithological references here and we saw little evidence that J.C.'s Francophile facial expressions and Gallic shrugs to any conversation every assisted him at parties to attract members of the opposite sex. Perhaps it also had to do with the foul-smelling Gauloise brand of cigarettes which he insisted on smoking as part of his affectation.

I had seen J.C. wearing army uniform one night as he sneaked quietly away to his usual Thursday night parade and I knew that as he was a year younger than I, he had probably joined up to escape the draft. So be it. I had no problems with this motive to serve the country. When we were alone and the other rowdies had taken off to join the drinking set at the Statesman's Rest for a few pints, I approached him about my chances of also joining the C.M.F. He was naturally overjoyed with having a fellow hostelista join him in his secret military activities. And so, on the next Thursday night, we both stole quietly out of the hostel, he in uniform and me in my teacher's garb hoping to make a good impression on his superior officers, Grand High Poohbahs (Military Division) at his barracks.

The barracks so the drill hall was called, was in the middle of the local, and at that time, the only university of the city. This was because it was an out company of a socially-acceptable university regiment way to our north in Sydney. Now a military Company usually consists of from eighty to one hundred and fifty men and is usually commanded by a major or at least a captain. It would have from three to six Platoons of thirty-three men, each under the command of a Lieutenant. Our little out company had only about forty personnel under the command of one lieutenant, one sergeant and several corporals; barely enough to make up one full platoon. There was also no regular army cadre staff – members of the regular army who were attached to a unit to provide professional administration and advice. In the midst of the affluent and well-coiffured national capital, the National Capital out company of the socially-acceptable Regiment looked rather inadequate and forlorn.

I was given a wad of official-looking documents which went under the group title of Recruitment Papers which included a medical form which was required to be filled in by one of the many GPs listed in an Appendix. This was at the Army's expense and was to ensure that during my training I would not to succumb to some medical deficiency which would cause the Army any distress and undue expense. The rest of the forms, all in triplicate, demanded a great deal of personal information which, if I was accepted, would be entered into the files of the Department of Defence for ever.

I dutifully found a local GP for my Army medical exam and made an appointment. His surgery was in the local and only shopping mall in the city. The doctor asked me all of the usual embarrassing questions about communicable diseases I might likely spread to the Armed Forces, noted that I had two arms and legs and could answer questions with a reasonable degree of understanding. Finally, he gave me a 500-millilitre beaker and requested a specimen. As his consulting room was only slightly bigger than a telephone booth with a reception desk outside in the corridor of the Mall, he suggested that I go to the public toilet to supply this specimen of urine. With a bit of searching, I finally found the public toilets; they were as far from the doctor's office as architecturally possible; there was an entire mall full of Saturday-morning shoppers between me and the medico. Oh well. The sacrifices which must be made for one's country! There had been a few worried looks by another occupant of the public toilets who was washing his hands when I wander in with a large glass beaker in hand but I found a cubicle and was able to pass a good supply of amber fluid. Now to run or at least walk with some dignity, the gauntlet back to the surgery.

Whilst the Poohbahs in the Department of Defence analysed the top secret nature of my recruitment papers and the analysed results of my amber fluid and associated medical report, I attended parades every Thursday with J.C. and went through the motions of training with five other new recruits; all of whom seemed to be younger than I and keen to keep out of the draft – not in the drill hall but that sweeping the entire country.

Eventually, Lieutenant Adams, our glorious leader happily announced that I had been accepted into their ranks and that a supply of my uniform and equipment would probably happen within the week or whenever a truck could be sent from H.Q. with the company's necessary supplies. Eventually, a month later, the other recruits and I were lined up by Sergeant Bozoni, our senior and only Sergeant, and presented with a table having various piles of clothing and equipment.

Boots – troops for the use of. One pair, black.

Gaiters – one pair, black.

Battle Dress Jacket – khaki, one.

Battle Dress Trousers – khaki, one.

Beret – black, one.

Hats – khaki fur felt, one

And so, the list went on until all recruits were standing like paralysed dress-makers dummies holding a pile of clothing, boots, webbing, water bottles, small canvas pack and other items. All looked like they had come out of a Second World War movie and indeed some of the labels had dates stamped in the 1940's. Now we were equipped to take on the nation's enemies, especially the ferals on the street corner. All we had to do was to work out how all of it was put together and worn with some sort of dignity. In a relatively short time, I was able to sneak out of the hostel on a Thursday night looking almost identical to J.C. My protest was complete.

Unfortunately, like the earnest anti-war protesters who had been swamped by the feral rent-a-crowd factions, my protest fell on deaf ears, or rather general disinterest. The few times which I had wandered the street around our drill hall in uniform had received little of a response. There were a few of the ferals attending the surrounding university campus who snarled and made a few cryptic gestures with their fingers, but most did not pay attention to my drab uniform and unmilitary posture. People were just not interested in the local military scene, especially of those who had joined the C.M.F.

Our Thursday night parades were hardly intensive courses in the gentle art of warfare. With only one officer and sergeant and three corporals, there only the basics of training. This consisted of learning how to stand, march, turn, and all of the other bodily functions which the army insisted on all its personnel performing. The drill on Saluting Officers received only a brief mention from Sergeant Bozoni who had a natural contempt for that class. Our lone officer, Lieutenant Adams was O.K. in his books, however. He was after all, really just another fellow university student who had more military experience and had somehow gained a commission. My colleagues of the company often called him by his nickname of Gomez which had come from his Latin looks (no doubt on his mother's side) and from his surname. The Addams Family was currently a popular television family with Gomez Addams being the patriarch of that dysfunctional family.

It was not uncommon, before our Thursday night parade, for newly-arrived soldiers to greet their popular commander by "Gidday, Gomez" with hardly a salute in sight. Gomez, himself took little note of such greetings as they were never done with any disrespect but with familiar respect. It was only during the more formal part of the parade and if by chance there was a visiting officer from the local gentlemen's Military Academy, that salutes were performed. Then they were frequent and of the Brigade of Guards crispness. We knew how to salute officers; we just did not see the need for it unless there was the need to show respect where it was earned.

Poor Gomez had the task of giving us the more detailed and theoretical lectures which were part of the Training Program which had come down from upon high. That being the Regimental Training Officer from Sydney. Unfortunately, at that time, the C.M.F. was equipped with leftovers from previous wars. We had the army's standard S.L.R.s or 'self-loading rifle' but our few Owen submachine guns were distinctly Second World War and often showed their age. Of course, being C.M.F. the army did not trust us with any ammunition, even blank ammunition, so all of our rifle drill involved the final word BANG after the order to "fire one round!".

Our training pamphlets, the army's version of individual training manuals were also of this vintage and often the instructions therein were rather archaic. I remember one lecture on Movement in the Field which exhorted solders to make maximum use of hedgerows for concealment when moving down country lanes. Finding the time of day in the field often referred to 'the village church tower clock'. As if any of these would be in working order! And so, our training waffled along with little excitement but with the best that Gomez and Bozo, our artificially gruff sergeant Bozoni, could perform. We were an out company which was somewhat like a frontier posting in the old days of the colony with little support nor care from our illustrious socially-acceptable regimental HQ in Sydney.

One saving grace of being a small out company in the nation's capital was our tenuous liaison with the local gentlemen's Military Academy. This august academy was the nation's prestigious training establishment for the officers of the Regular Army. It was established in 1911, just ten years after the nation had been put together from a loose and often antagonistic group of colonial states. It was equivalent to the United Kingdom's Sandhurst and West Point of the United States and was still only a gentlemen's club as female Officer Cadets were trained elsewhere and then only as a minority necessity as nurses, communications and administrative personnel.

On a few rare occasions, probably during semester breaks of the student body, the instructors at the gentlemen's Military Academy would invite our motley crew over for a guest lecture on some more technical matter because they had all of the latest training equipment such as armoured vehicles, howitzers and other stuff useful in warfare. They also had a rifle firing range for practicing the other useful skill such as shooting. This was well out of the city limits but within their military training grounds.

One Thursday night, Gomez excitedly announced that we were going to have a range day at the gentlemen's Military Academy's rifle range. Great excitement all round! We recruits looked at our rifles with some new feeling of attachment and usefulness. Our HQ in Sydney had managed to obtain some ammunition from the Regular Army after filling in a truckload of paperwork, all in triplicate, and it was being delivered by truck the following Thursday. The Commanding Officer of the gentlemen's Military Academy had reluctantly allowed our company to use the cadet's Rifle Live Firing Range (as it was called by them) for a weekend shoot. Bozo organised all of the extra paperwork, all in triplicate, for additional training on that weekend and all were expected to attend. Even the few of our more reluctant soldiers, who had joined to do their minimum 33 days per year in order to escape the draft, showed some new interest.

Thursday night came with a rush, as did all new and exciting events. Only Thursday fortnightly pay packets seemed to be as slow as a long weekend in the nation's capital. We were On Parade. That is, we had been ordered, as was the custom each parade, to get into formal ranks of three ready for the entry of our grand high commander, Gomez.

"O.K. Ya' Bastards. Get into line" Bozoni had ordered in his artificially gruff sergeant's voice. We had all got into our three ranks and our dressing, or relative positions, had been ordered so now we stood in three ranks and looked almost like soldiers.

"Right!" our sergeant continued. "I'll have three volunteers!" Without a second breath he looked at J.C. and me.

"Bottomly, Shipley and Puzzoso. You'll do! See me after Parade. I've got some useful things for you to do and some extra excitement."

After we had all been dismissed from the usual Thursday night's parade, Bozo called us over.

"Well, lads!" he said in his normal voice which often contained some friendly terms. "We have been given the honour of securing the range and you three will have the pleasure of attending the firing range and guarding it tomorrow night whilst we work our guts out here getting the ammo ready."

"Why us, Lord?" was a short prayer said by the three of us 'volunteers' in unison. J.C. had just done his Corporal's Exam so this would be his first test of leadership. Luigi and I were new recruits so there would be little protest from us. We all knew that the we part of Bozo's pronouncement did not include himself. He would be back here at the drill hall supervising the sleepover and sorting of the newly arrived ammunition. He would probably be in charge as Gomez had Friday night lectures to attend at the university where he studied Politics, the most common course in this city of aspiring politicians and public servants. No doubt Bozo would set everything (being our three corporals) in motion and then retire to Gomez's office to read the sporting pages for the weekend's races.

Everyone showed up on time on Friday evening. This was surprising as Friday nights were considered THE social night of the nation's capital. Teachers, including myself would usually hit the Suncrest Lounge at the Statesman's Rest hotel at 4 pm exactly and would get an early start. The public servants, including QANGO's and other supernumerary occupations, including the Drinking Set from my hostel would drift in about five thirty.

One drank until about six then there would be a lull in proceedings as some weaved their way home for dinner. Some of these, such as the hostel Drinking Set would eventually find their way back to the main bar afterwards for some serious drinking until ten when the hotel, and indeed the whole city shut down.

The three musketeers, or more technically correc, riflemen, carried their dispensed weekend equipment and threw it into the back of our unit truck. This was another relic, more modern than most, having seen active service in the Korean War only some fifteen years ago. Wheels Jones was our Corporal-Driver, having had the sense to take a driving course in the previous year. This he told us with a wink and a nod, was an easy cop as it meant that his duty during the usual cold, wet bivouac out in the distant scrub was guarding the truck from a nice warm stretcher in the back. He seemed to spend most of his time planning on different ways of making the back of this ancient vehicle into a cosy place of habitation. He had a camp stretcher, extra mattress and blankets in the rear of the truck and a camp cooker, jack rations, or non-military food items and the odd bottle or two stashed away in the truck's large tool box.

Relegated to the cold rear of the truck we sat as close to the rear tailgate as possible so that we could leer or show indifference to the civilians in following cars, depending upon their gender. Suitably seated, Wheels drove the truck out of the barracks and into the wild and circular roads of Friday night traffic. It was only a short distance of less than twenty minutes and a few gate stops at secret locations before we eventually arrived at our destination. This was somewhere west of the city within the gentlemen's Military Academy's huge training area and in the middle of a dark, grassy paddock.

"Out ya get!" cried Wheels as he suddenly appeared at the back of the truck and dropped the tailgate for us to debus. The army used this term for troops getting out of any object having wheels, whether it was a real bus, armoured personnel carrier or battered vintage truck.

"So long, guys. See ya in the mornin'" he yelled with a grin from his nice warm truck cab. Outside, here in the wilderness of the gentlemen's Military Academy Firing Range, it was beginning to get cold and an icy wind was blowing off the snow from Mount Franklin to the southwest of the city. It was after all, winter in this part of the world.

The army was ever mindful of such possibilities and had issued us with cotton combat uniforms; our nice warm wool Battledress being reserved for more formal events. Luckily our issue also included a thin jumper and best of all our heavy woollen greatcoat. This was a great issue. It was made out of thick material and covered most of the body when buttoned up to the chin. Similar coats had been worn by armies for centuries but now we thought more of Napoleon's retreat from Moscow and his miserable lines of similarly greatcoated troops trudging through the snow. We had no snow on the ground as yet, but the weather was such that we felt that it could fall at any moment.

We tramped around for a while until Louey found a deep, dry creek bed which gave us some respite from the icy wind that the national capital was noted for in its cold winters. Having had some self-training in field survival techniques during previous bivouacs, we gathered some dry wood and soon had a small fire going. This was supposed to be a tactical exercise with troops lying stoically on the cold ground waiting for the enemy to stupidly appear and blunder into our ambush. Blow that! It was cold and we were cold and so tactics went out the non-existent window.

We had each been issued a ration pack for our night's guard duty in securing the range. This was relatively generous as the ration was for an entire day. It was not long before we had a dixie of boiling water ready for a good, hot cup of tea.

"Hey! Wait-a minute!" Louey exclaimed. "I'va somethin' here that is good. Ay?" he said in his Italian English. Luigi came from Queanbeyan, the poor city just across the national capital's border with New South Wales, its surrounding state.

Louey pulled out a large, brown beer bottle from his Greatcoat. "It'sa Grappa that mi Nonno made ata home." He explained. "Rinsa outa your cups with a liddle and we try some. Yes?"

Louey pulled out the cork from the bottle and poured a little into my metal mug which had previously contained the strong, sweetened army tea. I swirled it around and threw it onto the fire. There was a sudden flash of blue flame as the strong spirit ignited. Wow! Was that a good home brew or what? Eagerly, J.C and I received our portion of Louey's grandfather's Grappa. This was strong stuff and excellent antifreeze. The night passed very well indeed, and the cold never seemed to bother us for some reason or other until the early morning dawn suddenly arrived.

Still externally frozen and feeling like I had been sleeping on rocks, which I had, I found my aching head and rekindled our small fire. The others finally came to with various groans and an oath from J.C. that he would never drink Grappa again, we set about having our sumptuous army ration breakfast of tinned eggs, army hard cereal block and tea.

We peered out of our small creek bed and thankfully saw that our fictitious enemy had not invaded the firing range of the gentlemen's Military Academy and that all was secure. Well, at least now for the first few metres as there was the usual thick morning fog blanketing the entire area and in both directions along our protective creek bed. After breakfast, we quickly put out our fire and buried it under dirt and stones and sorted out our uniforms in which we had slept. We heard the mechanical labouring sounds of our truck approaching through the fog and so we quickly assumed the erect soldierly stance of good sentries with our rifles slung over our Greatcoated shoulders and eyes alert. Nice try!

The rest of our company slowly and painfully debussed from our battered old truck. They had had a hard night working in the drill hall stacking boxes, moving them into our storeroom and then moving them out again and stacking them in the drill hall. This double shuffle was a result of Bozo forgetting to check the contents of the boxes in the first place. Such a manoeuvre was commonplace in the army and was generally called Greatcoats. This rather sartorial term came from the lack of decisiveness which often came at the beginning of a day's training when the caring officer would order his men on a cold morning to put their greatcoats on against the cold morning air as they went out for the first parade of the morning. Usually this was about 6 am and the weather always seemed to be cold in army camps at any time of year, even in the middle of heat waves.

Now our colleagues tumble out of the old truck grumbling about the cold night spent on stretchers in the cold drill hall with only army rations to eat. At least they brightened up when they saw the forlorn trio who had guarded the precious range throughout a bitter night without even a camp stretcher for comfort. Some passed remarks of sympathy but others felt some comfort in knowing that there were others who suffered more. The effects of the grappa and the warm campfire (non-tactical) from the previous evening were beginning to fade.

'Volunteers' removed the boxes of weapons and ammunition from the far interior of our truck and our three corporals bustled around getting the weapons ready for the first shoot; the fog still swirling around their feet as our three light machine guns were set up on the long firing mound which had just appeared.

Nothing much other than the usual wondering about as we all tried to work out what was going on. Bozo walked smartly up and down the firing mound inspecting each gun and its new belt of 7.62 mm bullets which had been painstakingly constructed the evening before. Lieutenant Adams arrived in his car an hour later, having had to stop at his university hall of residence to pick up his bivouac gear which he had forgotten as usual.

It was well into the morning when an army staff car finally arrived and disgorged a neatly attired Regular Army major who was an instructor at the gentlemen's Military Academy and the 'volunteered' Range Officer for the day's activities. After a few mumblings sotto voice, which included the terms "bloody weekend warriors", "cold as a polar bear's nipple" and the usual prayer "why me Lord?", he made his way over to Gomez who was sitting on an box reading up on the army pamphlet on 'how to fire a GPMG' or 'General Purpose Machine Gun'. Startled at seeing a superior being emerging through the fog, Gomez dropped the pamphlet and jumped up throwing a reasonably accurate salute.

Things began to get formal after that. The major ordered the reorganisation of Bozo's organisation so that the guns were now further apart with Bozo attentively acknowledging his superior's orders with copious responses at each new finicky order. "Yes, sir, Yes, sir" ("three bags full, sir" under his breath).

Having been formed into three platoons, greatly understrength of about twelve men each, in lines behind each gun, the major took over.

"First man down!" he ordered and the first man in each line dropped to the ground.

"Load – one belt of one hundred rounds!" and the first man in each platoon loaded a belt of ammunition into his gun. This had been the first time that any of us below the rank of corporal had loaded our guns with anything other than practice ammunition. This was getting exciting!

"Cock the weapon!" ordered the major and the metallic sound of bolts slamming home came through the fog which had now cleared to give us about 20 metres of visibility.

"Watch your front!" came the order. This seemed rather superfluous as there was not a lot of a front to watch, only a vague whiteness of the morning fog which happily seemed to be slowly lifting.

"Fire when the target comes to bear!" the major ordered in a tone somewhat like an old British Naval Captain commanding his ship against the Spanish Armada.

The targets were about three hundred metres up the gentle slope of the large, grassed firing range. After an excruciatingly long wait with fingers outside of the gun's trigger guard, each of the 'first men' waited expectedly for their target to appear. When they did eventually fade into the early morning sunlight, there was a large mob of sheep in the foreground.

"Don't fire! Stand down!" yelled the panic-stricken major who half ran and half jumped along the firing mound waving his arms in the air. Private Puzzoso put his finger onto the trigger and thought of his Nonno who had been in the Resistance and had fought against Mussolini in the northern hills of his homeland. Lamb for dinner was his second thought. The rest of the company thought that this was a great joke but Gomez threw his cap down and joined the major in showing his frustration.

"Another day at the office" thought Bozo, chewing on a muesli bar extracted from a ration pack. He had seen this sort of SNAFU[3] many times before.

---

[3] SNAFU refers to "Situation Normal – All Fouled Up" or words to that effect!

# Chapter Four: Strategic Resupply

So far, my relationship with the Army had been a good one. I liked the training and new skills which I was learning even if the equipment and the training manuals were of a time gone passed. However, this was to receive a temporary setback at the end of my first year.

This was the time for our Annual Camp. It was eagerly anticipated by most of our company. Although some, especially those who had joined the unit to escape the draft saw it as yet another interruption in their lives. They had attempted to escape being called up and then probably being sent to Vietnam, by volunteering for six years' service. During that time, they had to serve at least 33 days and be 'efficient' for that time. Whatever that meant!

For me, Annual Camp was a chance to play soldier for an extended period of time and in new circumstances other than our drill hall and the occasional forays out into the local countryside. The only problem, was that it was a regimental exercise and we would have to go to our Sydney HQ and join the rest of the socially-acceptable regiment.

Another advantage was that the camp was to be in the January school holidays. As a teacher this was marvellous as I would be paid as a Private soldier as well as have my holiday pay. The camp would be a nice little earner over the vacation. It was also time off for university students so most of our company would not have to ask their employers for leave. Most were unemployed anyway and the army pay would also help them with their living expenses and tuition fees.

I was also now accepted in their midst as I had reluctantly started part-time university at the beginning of the year. Unfortunately, the only science courses in a university geared up for political and economic programs were Experimental Psychology and Mathematics. I had taken on the psychology course as it had some interest to me as a teacher of potentially delinquent children. Mathematics I had always disliked with a passion and so for the time being, that was going to be ignored. Experimental Psychology was interesting because it included one three-hour session of 'practical work' each week. Of course, we had to experiment on each other as the university did not wish to employ laboratory rats for these experiments for economic reasons and for safety purposes; I am not sure whether that was to help us or the rats. My favourite experiment so far had been the 'Effects of Alcohol on Human Reaction Times'. There had been two groups required for this experiment. One which was called the control group and they measured how fast their timing was in turning off a light which suddenly came on whilst drinking water. The other group which I had volunteered for, repeated this activity but drank whiskey instead of the water. Needless to say, the experimental group's reaction times suffered greatly even after a few drams. One of my colleagues in this group had found the professor's whiskey bottle and had a few too many drams. He had problems finding the button to turn off the light so his results (and his Practical Report) were considered 'invalid'.

So, back at the draughty drill hall late on Friday afternoon, when the few public servants in our company such as J.C., were finally released from their public servitude. We loaded up all of the boxes ready to depart for the unit's alma mater in Sydney and were issued with our rifles but no bolts; they were kept in a locked metal box with Gomez's gear.

We now had two trucks; our battered veteran and a highly polished newcomer being driven by a real Regular corporal from the Transport Corps. He had come from the small, and also out company of a transport company whose main function in the nation's capital was to drive the gentlemen of the Military Academy around to their various non-campus activities. He seemed to be a little put out that he had been detached to drive a scruffy lot of 'Weekend Warriors' – as he called us – all the way to Sydney, some two hundred miles to our north. Driving the gentlemen of the Military Academy was considered a respectable occupation as the clientele was of a more socially-acceptable class and after all, they were going to be real soldiers one day, even if they were going to be officers.

Gomez had loaded the 'relic' – our name for the veteran truck – with all of the training equipment, and the machine guns in their coffin-like boxes and most of the stores needed for our camp. One of our corporals and a depleted platoon would go with him and Wheels would drive, whilst the rest of the company and some other stores would go with the regularly aggravated Regular corporal in his highly polished truck.

The designated remainder, including myself, loaded up the other stores and our all of our personal gear into the back of the highly polished truck under the watchful eye of its driver.

"Wipe yer feet!" he said as the first of our company climbed up into the rear of the truck. Bozo threw his rather bulky pack, kitbag and webbing into the back of the truck and went to the front of the vehicle to join the driver. I wasn't sure which one of the two I felt sorry for. It was going to be a long journey and Bozo was a great talker.

We drove out of our 'barracks' leaving Wheels trying to start the Relic with a series of gear-wrenching screeches. We were on our way to Annual Camp at last.

There always seemed to be some romance in driving in the back of an army truck and the chance to leer or show indifference to the civilian population. No doubt my view would change after a two-hundred-mile trip over one of the most used and least maintained highways in the country. I guess it was because it was one of those rare moments when we felt like we were real military types.

Henry 'Flash' Gordon, one of our other three corporals sat at the end of the long side bench nearest the open end of the truck. He had been given that nickname for reasons other than that used by the space hero of comic books and movies. Flash was a used car salesman in Queanbeyan – the type who could always get you what you wanted wholesale; whether it was a car, expensive wristwatch or any other contraband. When he finished his Economics-Law Degree, he would most likely go on to become a politician – he would then have all of the essential qualifications. For all that, he was a good corporal and always looked after his squad in a no-compromise manner.

This trip was to be no exception to Flash's devious ways. The 'other stores', which he was in charge of loading on board this truck, consisted of the remainder of our supply of ration boxes. These had been kept in our back storeroom for a considerable time and Gomez had always forgotten to have them returned to Sydney. By now they had passed their 'establishment' date and so did not need to be accounted for in any of the army's paperwork (all in triplicate). Each box contained two rectangular metal canisters containing three or four 'Combat

Ration One Man' packs. There were five different varieties; labelled with some degree of indifference and gastronomic vagary as Rations A, B, C, D and E. All members of these varieties were generally hated by the troops who would sometimes supplement these with 'jack rations' brought from home and smuggled in empty ammunition pouches on our webbing. This was possible because we rarely had ammunition and the tastier food items gave the pouches some bulk and the appearance of performing their function. Of course, more officious young officers often inspected these pouches if the soldier concerned showed any nervousness on parade. They would be immediately confiscated and the offender given some additional duty in exchange. Such officers would naturally dispose of these items during his own meal breaks.

Napoleon Bonaparte was reported in saying that 'an army marches on its stomach' suggesting with a somewhat poor knowledge of the Human anatomy that an army goes well when well feed. Whether he actually said this or not, he certainly knew that well-fed troops marched a lot better than those who were not, especially in returning from a quick jaunt to Moscow in 1812.

Our army obviously had not heard of this maxim but relied more on what they thought the troops needed and what could be crammed into a small ration pack and thence into the soldier's backpack. Well, the army considered them nutritious but the troops certainly not think of them as delicious.

They contained the following:

| A | B | C | D | E |
|---|---|---|---|---|
| Ham & Egg | Pork & Beans | Luncheon Meat type II | Sausages & Veg | Beef & Egg |
| Jam, plum | Jam, raspberry | Jam, apricot | Jam, blackberry | Jam, peach |
| Curry powder | Curry powder | Curry powder | Soup Pdr, beef | Soup pdr, chicken |
| Beef & veg | Corned beef | Beef & gravy | Luncheon Meat type I | Corned beef |
| Dried rice | Dried rice | Dried rice | Potato & onion dried | Potato & onion dried |
| Peaches | Peaches | Pears | Two fruits | Two fruits |

These sumptuous items were either in small tins as in the meat dishes and fruit or in tooth-paste style tubes (olive drab colour).

Each pack also contained items common to all including: a cereal block; biscuits (2 packs survival); biscuits (shortbread); cheese (tin); chewing gum; butterscotch lollies; butter (tin); sweetened condensed milk (tube); sugar (12 sachets); teabags (2); instant coffee (2); salt (1 sachet); and fruit drink powder. They also contained a scouring pad, small soap cake, toilet paper (shiny smooth), waterproof matches and a most useful tin opener/spoon called FRED.

This last item was perhaps one of the most useful things in the entire ration pack. FRED was the Field Ration Eating Device but was usually called a F***ing Ridiculous Eating Device instead. This was a short, stubby metal spoon which had a small flip blade for opening cans and a cut-away section at the end which could be used to open bottles. These were often horded by members of the C.M.F. as they proved to be very useful at home when the larger, electric can-opener failed.

In retrospect, the ration packs were not really that bad and really showed a lot of planning by the army's caterers. They were a novel item to us as we rarely had much field experience and we would diligently follow the green paper of instructions which came with each pack. Two packs would be issued for a weekend bivouac and there would be much trading if one did not like the items in our particular lettered pack which was issued.

The meat dishes came in cans like all previously issued army rations going back for many years and some unkind souls suggested that they came from the same source – probably a horse which had died in the Boer War. The canned cheese was also suspect as it was always very salty and eaten at midday with the biscuits (survival) and the juice powder which was sour and usually gave heartburn.

The cereal block was perhaps the hardest piece of 'hard tack' ever to be eaten (attempted only) by humankind. I am sure that even sailors of Nelson's navy would have rejected it. It was not until our first contact with 'veterans' at our Annual Camp that we found that this indigestible block with brick-like qualities could be made into a really nice porridge. This culinary secret started with the cereal block being added to one's metal mug at the close of the evening meal with the last drops of hot water being added from the metal dixie or boiling container which came with the water bottles. This was allowed to soak overnight. The next morning, sweetened condensed milk was added and also some of the jam.

Sugar to taste and a little more boiling water to build the consistency up to a porridge. Lovely. Well, it was warm and tasty on any cold morning!

Many of the other items also showed some promise; the tubes of sweetened condensed milk and jams were of considerable attraction. They were convenient to use and could be applied for a wide range of application from spreading on the hard tack 'biscuits survival' to making a reasonable porridge with the cereal block. Like everything else in the pack except the biscuits and some other small packets, they were in tubes coloured 'jungle green' and so one had to place them in a conspicuous place when eating least they be lost in the grass. The toilet paper was a waste of time as it had a shiny, non-absorbent surface and so it was like using a plastic bag when one wanted to go.

As we were loading the highly polished truck with our 'other stores', Bozo sauntered past and watched us load the boxes into the rear of the truck.

"You lucky bastards!" he remarked. "I've got some good news and some bad news for ya! What do ya want first?"

"Give us the bad news." said 'Sorrowful' Higley, the unit pessimist.

"Well," Bozo continued, pushing his giggle hat to the back of his bald head, "Yer are havin' ration packs for dinner, tonight."

"What's the good news?" asked Sorrowful.

"There's plenty of them!" laughed Bozo, pushing his hat down over his forehead and walking away laughing.

There was no doubt that such a comment also meant that Bozo had stashed his ammunition packs with enough jack rations to last the trip and our aggravated Regular would have the usual army truckies' supply of 'goodies' in the highly polished truck's tool box.

On the road now and our aggravated Regular driver did his best to annoy the smaller vehicles of the Friday night city traffic by tailgating as many small cars as possible and at the highest speed that the local police would allow. We were content just to leer and show indifference to the drivers in the cars following us, holding our rifles in the upright, wary, position in full view.

Having expertly negotiated the many concentric circles and spokes which made up the nation's capital inner road network, we got onto the federal Highway heading north. This was a nice patch of smooth, federally-funded highway which would soon give way to the bumpy, pot-hole infested surface of the Hume Highway which was state funded.

Flash decided it was time for dinner so he order Louey and Sorrowful to break out the rations. Most of the uni students and public servants were yet to eat and people like me who had had lost our chance to have food at our hostel were still hungry. The cardboard cartons were pulled open, the metal canisters removed and the packs handed round in the darkness. Which lettered menu we were given was the luck of the draw and there was very little light in the rear of the truck. Soon, small pocket torches, an illegal but indispensable item for bivouacs, began to illuminate the type of pack and its content.

"Damn!" came a voice from the darkened interior. "I have the beef and gravy! Anyone want to swap it?"

Considering that we were having to eat our meal cold, such an item seemed highly undesirable. Silence except for the sound of tyres on the road.

Flash seemed to take anything as he found it. In fact, he was noted for just taking anything if it wasn't nailed down. He sat content with his rifle jammed upright between his knees, a ration pack on his lap and was opening one of the larger cans.

"Corn beef! Good oh!" he exclaimed and used his FRED to opening his prize. He was soon eagerly devouring his beloved corned beef.

I had found that I had scored a Ration Pack Type B which was good enough because it had canned peaches as desert. The corned beef was acceptable, although it tended to have copious lumps of white congealed fat mixed in with the meat. Biscuits Shortbread covered with the raspberry jam and water from my canteen was going to be my poor repast. The rest of the ration pack would just have to wait for its disposal.

Flash seemed to be newly animated at the tailgate of the truck. A yellow Volkswagen 'Kombi' van with hand painted slogans and surfboards on top had pulled in close behind us. We all moved up to see what was going on. The contents of the 'Kombi' were a group of surfers travelling north to get some wave time in on one of Sydney's long beaches. They initially resembled our ferals from the city's protest marches, but these were a greatly modified species. Hair was long. True, but it was generally bleached blonde and they had a healthier-looking tanned face rather than the pale and spotty faces of our ferals. Their dress was also a lot more colourful and seemed to be devoid of slogans and generally intact.

The passenger was eagerly pointing to Flash's ration pack and held up a can of beer other than the one he was drinking. They all were drinking beer, including the driver, and the group in the back seat gave a hearty raised-can salute in support of their leader in front. Flash got the message in a flash. Never slow to miss an opportunity, he put his rifle down and motioned that the van should pull up to the side of truck as if to overtake. This would bring their passenger window almost level with the tailgate of the truck.

This manoeuvre completed, and with Flash leaning out of the rear of the truck being held by his belt by one of our team, the almost complete ration pack was successfully thrown into the window of the Kombi. A full can of beer returned. Transfer complete.

The boys in van ripped open the rest of Flash's ration pack and eagerly inspected its contents. What a treasure! Army green tubes and khaki packets of all sorts of new and wondrous items. They were exited.

The boys in the back seat rummaged in the back of the van and brought up the remains of a slab of beer cans. What a treasure! We all thought and hurried to grab the remains of our ration packs. Soon there was an alternate throwing of ration packs and beer cans until the beer ran out. Never mind, we had enough for half a can of very welcome cold amber fluid to supplement our cold evening meal. With a final wave and a toot of the van's horn, our benevolent surfers finally continued to overtake our highly polished truck, much to the annoyance of our aggravated Regular driver. Strategic resupply complete.

## Chapter Five: Stalag Bandicoot

It was fast approaching midnight as our truck slowly ground to a shuddering halt. We had finally arrived at the army training camp at Bandicoot Hill on the far western outskirts of Sydney. We could have been anywhere for all it mattered as we slowly roused ourselves from the intermittent periods of dozing which some may have mislabelled as sleep.

True to his character, some sixth sense had roused Flash as we had turned into the camp's driveway and so he got up and stumbled his way across the jumbled bodies which had tried to make themselves comfortable in their greatcoats on the bare wooden floor of a bouncing army truck. He quickly resumed his position of leering and indifference at the end of the bench near the tailgate and put an empty can of beer to his lips. Just as our aggravated Regular appeared to drop down the tailgate, Flash appeared to be going through the last act of sculling the last drop of beer from his can.

The tailgate and the Reg's jaw both dropped at the same time. Instead of the usual greeting of "rise and shine you dozy diggers!" all he could say incredulously was:

"Where'd you get tha beer from?"

Flash gave him a secretive wink and replied with a smirk "We're C.M.F. mate! Soldiers and Civilians. We have skills which you Regs will never know of." And with that he jumped down off the truck, grabbed his gear and stood the empty beer can on the deck of the truck.

In the rear of the truck, the rest of us had come to and had witnessed Flash's little ploy so as we got to the tailgate, those who had them also placed their empty beer cans next to that of our dodgy Corporal.

It was cold for a midsummer's night as it always seemed to be in any army camp. The army must go to extraordinary lengths to find locations which were either cold or extremely hot for the extra training value of their troops.

I looked around through half-closed sleepy eyes at the darken buildings which ran in ordered lines off into the even darker night. I had a weird feeling of déjà vu which I could not quite understand but I picked up my pack and threw it over one shoulder and grabbed my webbing and kitbag in hand and wandered over to the side of the road where our little group were attempting to form into some sort of military formation resembling two ranks.

Bozo had wandered even more aimlessly from the front cab of the truck and looked at the beer and the open-mouth and now very aggravated Regular driver. He too was wondering where we had acquired this strategic resupply but kept quiet as Flash brushed past and slipped a full can of beer into his hand.

"No names, no pack drill," Flash had whispered as he brushed past.

The aggravated Regular driver had finished scratching his head and went into the guard house to look for the Officer of the Guard. The lone sentry at the gate in his greatcoat and rifle with bayonet fixed, had come out of semi-comatose watchfulness had wandered into the entry way to wonder about the newcomers. He promptly about faced and put on an air of alertness when our driver and a rather disassembled Second Lieutenant came out of the guardhouse. The young officer was not happy to have been woken up from his warm camp stretcher in the Guardhouse and was not completely with it. Most Second Lieutenants always seemed to be this way even in the middle of the day. He signed the driver's delivery papers with a tired hand and wandered over to Bozo who had seen him coming and had pulled his uniform together and put on his giggle hat and now looked something like a sergeant. Our driver, still shaking his head and trying to solve the great beer supply mystery climbed back into his truck and drove off down the road towards his billet for the night.

Having been signed for by the young Second Lieutenant, we were now officially part of our socially-acceptable regiment. As a small and thoroughly under-strength regiment, we also consisted of only one combat unit or battalion. Some bigger regiments in the Regular Army have several battalions per regiment, but we were C.M.F. and our recruiting numbers had dropped overall, even with those soldiers who had joined up to escape the draft. As the socially-acceptable regiment's out company we had been designated as D or Delta Company had theoretically had three platoons each of one officer, one sergeant, one radio operator/batman and three sections of ten men consisting of a corporal, nine soldiers and one light machine gun. Our actual numbers were about fifty to seventy-five percent of those numbers.

The dreary Second Lieutenant muttered something to our sergeant-in-command, Bozo, and extended a limp wrist down the road into the darkness.

"Huts 23, 24 and 25. Down there somewhere," he said with a tired yawn and gave a feeble return to Bozo's Guard-like salute and wandered back into the Guardhouse. Bozo could play the efficient sergeant when it was necessary.

"O.K. you lot! Snap to it!" he ordered in a loud voice designed to wake up the rest of the guard and anyone else within hearing range. "Pick up your gear. Left turn. Quick march!" The last part of the order was for sound effect only so we picked up our packs and webbing and threw them over one shoulder, grabbed our kit bags and sauntered off in some sort of double file. This soon degenerated into a gaggle as usual when there were no officers present.

Most of us were already asleep on our feet by the time we arrived at Huts 23, 24 and 25. Bozo halted the gaggle and told us in a much quieter voice that there were others sleeping in the other huts and so we were to be quiet and get some sleep ourselves.

Reveille was at six. Oh, well. Six hours sleep wasn't too bad!

Each of the huts was designed for a platoon so we would have plenty of rooms to choose from. Up the three steps and into the long wooden block which had a long corridor of bare planks with rooms off on each side. Flash and his two corporal cronies took the first three rooms and the rest of us wandered into which ever one was vacant.

"No lights!" Bozo had said but luckily some moonlight filtered through the dirty wire mesh of the uncurtained window opposite to the doorway. I was too tired to care much and so I threw my gear down onto the floor and released the rolled-up, shiny mattress that sat at the head of a rather uncomfortable-looking tubular steel and wire bed. There was a pile consisting of a rather stained, striped pillow topped with two folded brown blankets at the foot of the bed. I was too sleepy to search in my kit bag for my pyjamas so I stripped to my underwear, donned my greatcoat and crawled between the two blankets. The mattress below had a cold, vinyl covering but at least it was soft. Sleep came instantly, despite the cold mattress and the feeling that I had been here before.

Sleep was temporarily interrupted as the Relic pulled into camp with a high-pitched squealing of brakes and the noises associated with Gomez and the rest of our Company going through the usual arrival ritual in waking up the young Lieutenant of the Guard. This was soon followed by feet thumping down our corridor and the usual shuffling of boots, clothing and the making of beds. Soon all lights were out and the chronic snorers given a chance to exercise their lungs.

The morning was broken by some lunatic blowing a bugle. The sun had barely climbed slowly over the distant horizon down the hill from our huts and it was still cold. I looked out the bare, open window to see the next hut in our numbered sequence and to hear sounds of cursing as the rest of my platoon became aware that reveille was upon us. Much too early we all thought.

It was only in the harsh light of the early morning bugle-blowing reveille that my memory finally gave up its recall of where I had seen my new quarters before. This was my room back at my hostel in the nation's capital! There was the same long line of wooden buildings raised up on short stilts, the long corridors lined with doors which led into drab, light green-painted rooms with the ubiquitous faded floral linoleum. My new room, however lacked most of my furniture, having only a metal, tubular framed bed and a stark dark blue metal storage cupboard. It was likely that somewhere back in the nation's capital there was a planning section of the Department of Administrative Administration which contained such secret plans for army barracks and government hostels. No other government building seemed to have this basic plan. Well! I hoped that the food was better!

I was soon to find out. Reveille had been at six sharp and we all tumbled out of Huts 23, 24 and 25 and formed up as a forlorn group in three shabby ranks for early morning Sick Parade. This was the army's version of a head count and muster by platoons. There were no uniform regulations for such a parade, but most of my colleagues were dressed in a similar manner to what we had slept in; underwear, greatcoat, boots without laces, and hats Khaki Fur Felt.

Bozo sauntered out of his hut and stood in front of our platoon whilst our other two sergeants in more mundane greatcoat, boots and Hats KF uniform took their places in front of the other two platoons. Bozo attempted to look like an efficient sergeant but with bright pink pyjama trousers showing from under his greatcoat, the effect was somehow lost.

The roll was taken which did not take very long with our depleted numbers; the men answering "yes Sergeant!" as their names were called. No one reported sick so we were sent back to get ready for the morning Breakfast Parade. Those that felt that they needed it, myself included, wandered down in our underwear, greatcoats and boots unlaced but now a towel over the shoulder had replaced the Hats KF. The shower block down the tarred road also had similarities to that facility back at the hostel. The floor was cold, bare concrete and the shower and toilet cubicles backed on to the outside walls which, like their side walls only started about a foot off the ground and finished about another foot from the start of the roof. There was no ceiling as such, only the arched roof of cobweb-draped corrugated iron. The water temperature coming from the rusty rosettes varied from lukewarm to cold. At least my hostel facilities had hot water.

Promptly at seven we were back on parade in our three platoons clean, well most anyway, and in our 'Greens' uniform with polished boots, with army Khaki socks this time, but no Hats KF nor black belt. We also had to carry our army mug as tea cups and saucers were considered too civilized for the 'Rank-and-file. All ready for breakfast, we were given an order 'Turn to the right in threes; right turn' and then marched up the hill towards the long building near the front gate which was the Mess Hall. Other similar lines of men also were coming from other hut areas and joining us on the road. This was something new! A regimental breakfast! Well, almost! Their Company ranks seemed to be as depleted as ours. There were only corporals marching by the side of these serpentine groups as the officers would no doubt awaken from their slumbers soon and find their way to the Officers' Mess; a more freshly-painted building with a pretend lattice pergola on one side which was separated from our mess by the Guardhouse. They would be allowed civilized cups and saucers and would not have to bring their mugs with them, after all, they were gentlemen. We wondered if Gomez had survived the auditory attack of the bugler and was only now getting ready for a good morning repast. Our sergeants would have by now wandered into the Sergeants and Non-commissioned Officers Mess which was further along from ours. They would, no doubt, have everything sorted out; being long-practiced in modifying army conditions. No cups and saucers for them! They would have their own individual china mugs with appropriate personal slogans written on each.

Our short march was terminated in a March Easy with the usual gaggle as men jostled from three ranks into single file at the door of the Mess Hall. It too, was nothing flash; just a long hall with two sets of temporary tables – Tables Field Service – they were called, or just Tables FS with simple, foldable wooden chairs lined along each side. The central aisle led down to the Servery Area which, like our hostel back in the nation's capital consisted of a long line of counters with raised shutters. As if to add to the impression of being home, the cooks standing ready behind these counters with the large pots of food also had a strong resemblance to those of the hostel. I expected cigarettes hanging from their mouths and dirty fingernails grasping ladles, but at least the army had some hygiene standards which our young Lieutenant would have had the dubious pleasure of previously inspecting, the kitchen, the food, the cooking pots and the cooks' fingernails.

We moved along the line of counters with our thin metal trays and plates which we had picked up at the start of the queue. A similar process to the hostel. As we approached each cook, an item of food would be unceremoniously slopped onto our plate. There was a choice of eggs this morning; this one or that one. The eggs were fried or poached or somewhat in between, well that had been the aim initially but somehow, they only looked half cooked. The white was its appropriate colour but with that gelatinous texture which suggested only partial cooking. The yoke looked up at us with a healthy yellow glow, but it too looked very runny. For some reason, probably to stop the gelatinous eggs from escaping, they all were sitting on slices of white bread. Interesting! The eggs were lifted off their soft, white beds by a flattened lifter and slopped onto the plate. I imagined that, like their counterparts back at the hostel, the cooks would later use the rafts of white bread in some form of bread-and-butter pudding.

This at least would be a welcome sight as armed-forces B & B pudding usually tasted quite nice, especially if spiced with raspberry jam out of the jungle-green tubes from Ration Type B.

Long, limp sausages were next in line. Two each per man perhaps was the standard army ration. They were fairly tasteless and had a remarkably uniform texture of meat from some unspoken source which had been ground almost to a microscopic pulp. This was followed at the next counter by two more rationed rashers of thin, very greasy bacon.

A generous dollop of baked beans completed this morning's sumptuous breakfast.

Of course, there was the ubiquitous table of cereal, jugs of milk and very large pots of tea and coffee sitting on a table FS in the far corner. The central tables had been set with solid, dull military silverware, sturdy plates and bowls of white crockery all bearing the logo of the nation in faded blue. In the centre of each table was a single cluster of condiments arranged very much like a circle of wagons waiting for the inevitable attack. Army tinned butter, HP and tomato sauce, metal bowls of white sugar and packets of equally white bread made up the larger group. Holding pride of place within the centre of each group was a jar of vegemite and a tin of the legendary army lemon spread. The latter was quite tasty in a tangy way and the white bread, butter and spreads helped out if the main food items were too much for the stomach. Army tea and coffee were made as strong as the black grease used on army trucks.

After breakfast, we ambled back to our lines in small groups. The fellows from other companies which we had met at the breakfast table seemed a good bunch. On the way back, we met Bozo also ambling from the Sergeants' Mess.

"Get a move on, you lot! Parade in fifteen minutes!" he called, trying to act like a real sergeant.

We decided that our new and more formal location in Stalag Bandicoot, the name that the others at our table had referred to our new home, warranted some respect for Bozo's new-found efficiency, so we got a move on, and walked quickly back to our lines.

A quick repolish of our black boots, gaiters and belt and a little straightening out of the wrinkles in our uniform and we were ready for action. One by one, we grabbed our rifle and extracted its bolt from its hiding place. We were not supposed to keep the rifles in shooting order, so when not in use their bolts, a complex piece of iron-mongery about four inches long, was to be put out of sight. This term meant that it could not be found by devious sergeants or officers who inspected our lines each morning. The idea being that rifles and their bolt should stay parted until they were needed in case some militant feral or more organised criminal wandered into the base and stole our weapons. This morning being our first was the only exception. Dozy Diggers, the general name for incompetent and foolish soldiers, would keep them in a top pocket of their shirt; a very obvious place as seen by the misshapen bulge, and would soon be spotted. Not a good look and not a great hiding place. Other in the Almost Dozy category would hide their bolts in the metal press which pretended to be a wardrobe. They would probably lay it out alongside their toothpaste tube and brush, but as these and every other item in the press had its military position and orientation, it would soon be spotted by even the sleepiest of Second Lieutenants. Sergeants knew everything so this would be the second place, after the shirt pocket, that they would look. Old hands at this game found more enlightened places to hide their bolts; inside their upturned army mug in its regimental place on the second shelf was a good place as it was very convenient but had to be removed to a secondary place, say inside the toiletries bag when going to breakfast. Under the pillow was another dozy place for the bolts during breakfast as this would be the third place that sergeants would look. It was common to return from breakfast to find some grinning three-striper waiting at the steps of a hut holding a bag of bolts. After a quick bucketing about our collective stupidity and the award of some extra duty for the hut, we would have to then sort out which bolts belonged to which rifle by referring to its number stamped on its side. These should match those on the side of the rifle and we were expected to remember an eight-digit number as well as our own Army Number.

So, having bolted up our rifles and bolted down the corridor into the light of day, we assembled in our platoons in three ranks. Standing in the at ease position, we had time to look around, moving our eyes and not our heads so as not to spoil our military formation, we noticed that there were new officers standing in front of our platoon and the one next to us. Gomez had taken his position in front of the third platoon of our D-Company now resuming his place as a Platoon Commander rather than as de facto Company Commander back at our home barracks.

Bozo brought us to attention and did a quick head count then nodded with satisfaction that not one as yet had reported in sick with food poisoning after breakfast. He smartly about-faced and marched up to our new officer and gave an even smarter salute. This was a new Sergeant Bozoni which we would have to get used to. The officer returned the salute with a vague, limp-wristed raising of his arm and hand and took one step forwards. Sergeant Bozoni about faced with an uncharacteristic smartness, and marched around to his allotted position behind the platoon.

"Stand at…ease!" came the order from our new officer. "I am Second Lieutenant Arnott!" he exclaimed rather proudly. "I will be your Platoon Commander for the rest of the camp." He added. The voice came out as an attempt to show his lofty position over our assembled ranks. Lower in tone but higher in volume. Unfortunately, there was the occasional squeak and lisp in some of his words which suggested a bad omen for his future command of our platoon. This introduction was compounded by his appearance. Whilst his uniform was immaculate in every respect, especially the bright shiny new pips on each of his shoulder boards, his stance and general appearance suggested that leadership was something unnatural to him. He was attempting to stand erect like an officer should at all times, but a pair of rounded shoulders made such a stance irrelevant. A few strands of bright red hair had strayed from below the peak of his cap and his face was perhaps the whitest that I had ever seen, save from photos of Japanese Kabuki players.

Later that night, in conversation with older hands, we found out that Second Lieutenant Arnott was called 2Lt Biscuit or just plain Biscuit depending upon the formality of the conversation. Of course, this name would never be used within his hearing range. Furthermore, it was discovered that he had recently graduated with a degree in accountancy and was now a junior member of Arnott, Arnott and Bleak, Accountants in the city. Young Arnott had yet to fully qualify so the company was not yet at the status Arnott cubed. Who Mr. Bleak was, was anyone's guess but he would probably be a relative and a former member of our socially acceptable regiment. It seemed that Gomez's preferred studies in politics and economics was well in line with regimental expectations, as a good number of the officers were accountants, actuaries and other such bean counters. It was apparently a good thing to have the socially- acceptable regiment's name on one's CV if applying to join companies such as Arnott, Arnott and Bleak. Our officer had an older brother, no doubt he was the second Arnott in the company's name, who was also captain in the regiment. He was soon identified by his rounded shoulders, red hair and pasty face but an older variation. We came to these conclusions when the older Arnott suddenly appeared and came up to his younger brother in some sort of amble – march. A bevy of limp-wristed salutes followed and Biscuit Senior about faced and wandered down to our left flank. He was obviously our new Company Commander. There was a command made from this august person:

"Delta Company will advance, Left turn!" and we did a left turn as smartly as we could. Biscuit Junior marched or ambled to the now front of our file of three and continued his command from there. Bozo had also moved to what was now the rear of our platoon. The command continued:

"Delta Company, by the Right, quick march!" and off we went down the road towards the large parade ground that was at the bottom of the camp.

"Left right, left right…" Bozo called out from the rear to keep us all in step. At this early stage such a feat was almost impossible as our column must have resembled a centipede with arthritis.

We detected an ominous presence over to one side of the column. With furtive eyes-only glances were saw a stiff, Non-commissioned Officer, marching rigidly off to our left. He had the rank of Warrant Officer Class Two on his sleeve and a long, polished pace-stick under his left arm, he was obviously our new Company Sergeant Major. His eyes seemed to be everywhere so we promptly resumed 'eyes front' and continued marching, with more effort to keep in step now, hoping that he would go away or at least not descend upon our platoon.

It was somewhat exhilarating to be in a full company march. Our efforts back in our own barracks in the nation's capital had only been minor affairs within our own perimeter. Marching outside with the university ground was tantamount to declaring war on the feral set of the student body. Now we were safely within the single-strand and rickety fences of the army camp at Bandicoot Hill so we could march with some confidence, albeit in the presence of the Company Sergeant Major.

Down the road and onto the verges of the parade ground we marched. There were three more caterpillars of men converging on the ground, but their legs seemed to be going in far better unison than ours. Eventually, Biscuit Senior gave the command to halt and we came to a shuddering stop, somewhat like a train of loose carriages arriving at a platform.

"Company, right turn!" came his command. "Attention!" This command was rather superfluous as we had stopped in that position. It was probably too early in the morning for him to remember such things. "Company, right dress!" and front and rear ranks took a step forward and to the rear as appropriate then the front rank quickly turned their heads to the right and brought up their left arms so that their fists sought out the shoulder of the next man to their right. On the command 'dress!' the platoons shuffled so that their ranks began to form into straighter lines than had been destroyed through their marching. On the command 'attention!' the arms came down and the heads snapped again to the front.

"Stand at ease!" Biscuit Senior ordered. Biscuit Junior, Gomez and the other as yet unnamed Second Lieutenant smartly marched around to stand in front of their platoon.

"Stand easy!" came the command and so we were able to relax without being seen to relax. This meant that were still kept our bodies erect, our head and eyes generally to the front, although some movement here was allowed, and we could breathe more easily. It was the usual position that bodies of men were put into when there was some anticipation of waiting. The other companies also had assumed this position and we waited. And waited. And waited some more.

Finally, about twenty minutes later, a little group of men with considerable brilliance of reflection coming off their large collection of brass pips and crowns, marched as a gaggle onto the parade ground. At their front was a rather large man in both height and girth. This was Lieutenant-colonel Willoughby, the regiment's colonel. He was known to all, by sight at least, as his smiling face beamed down from every company notice board, including our barracks. Lt-Col. John D. Willoughby had also been a graduate of the commissioning process of our socially-acceptable regiment and so had risen though its ranks over many years and had survived all of its hostile engagements. He had also survived the frantic world of accountancy and had become, against many odds, the C.E.O. of a major national company.

He had the reputation of being a 'soldiers' commander' and no doubt got to his high civilian position by knowing what went on in his company and who were its people. He was respected by all to the point that his epithet was simply 'Colonel Willoughby' usually in a more casual tone as 'The Colonel'. We later found that he would appear at any stage of our training as a 'casual visitor'. Of course, the sergeants or younger officers would jump up to attention and yell 'squad' or 'Platoon' or whatever group we were in so that we would all jump to attention, but the Colonel usually beat them to it with an 'at ease'. He would then talk to the group in a friendly manner, often speaking to some of the older hands by their rank and name. When he did this with D - company, which had been previously a list of names, ranks and serial numbers to him, he would ask our names and have a short conversation with us.

"Ah, Private Shipley", he said one morning as we had been caught trying unsuccessfully to camouflage ourselves in a copse of bushes, "You're a schoolteacher, I believe?" He had obviously looked up our records beforehand. He was a good leader of men and tried to run an efficient regiment; only the surfeit of young officers with nothing to do was his problem as the regiment trained its own officers yet had nowhere else for them to go.

The colonel, having gone through his short words of command to bring his regiment up to his attention and then set us all at 'stand easy', gave us a welcoming speech which was brief for such military speech, and then marched off with his retinue of Headquarters staff. Companies were then left in command of their Company Commanders who marched us all back to our respective lines to get ready for the day's training. Biscuit Senior handed over to Biscuit Junior and the other Platoon Commanders who then handed over to the Platoon Sergeants. Bozo had looked around to hand us over to someone else but our Corporals still stood at attention. Instead he stood us at ease and then stand easy and read out the plan for the day. It was like some restaurant menu but hardly appetising.

"First, we will have a charming little piece of close-order marching as a Company with the delightful Sergeant-major Strang." He read from a clipboard which had suddenly appeared. This was not received well as our new CSM. We had learnt at breakfast that he was another one of those hardened Ex-Regular soldiers who had transferred to the C.M.F. following many years' service as a professional soldier. Now he was confronted by a bunch of ex-civilians who were at best a bunch of well-meaning amateurs and at worst a C.S.M.'s nightmare. Bozo continued with his Italian menu of horrors:

"Next, following a salubrious cold-meat salad luncheon, we will break up into platoons and go through, by numbers of course, the delightful intricacies of disassembling and reassembling of the light machine gun with Staff Sergeant Butler" This was also not received well. 'Blousy' Butler, the fat Quartermaster and Armorer was a popular NCO but we had all been through this lesson back at our barracks many times.

Several more unpleasant or boring sessions were read out as 'main courses' and then for 'dessert' after another 'sumptuous dinner' of beef stew and real dessert of army custard, we would have an evening lecture by Second-Lieutenant Arnott on 'Water Resupply in the Field.' Excitement was the last emotion experienced by all at this abhorrent agenda of our daily tasks.

# Chapter Six: Watch Your Front...

And so, our daily training at Army Camp Bandicoot Hills, known unaffectionately to all as Stalag Bandicoot, went on to the point of daily boredom. It was either at Platoon level in which some tough drill sergeant exercised us in the many intricate manoeuvres of marching, turning, about turning, wheeling saluting, dressing, and more marching.

We did all of these tasks to numbers. It seemed that the army trained everyone in everything by numbers. It would start off with the ubiquitous phrase "For the purpose of training, the action is broken down in stages by numbers..." The instructor would then run through the action at the speed of light returning to his own stance of innocence and begin the numerical sequence. Weird thoughts often flowed through our minds whilst we were standing at ease on some small parade ground waiting for the instructor to show up. We imagined that our lecture that afternoon on Health and Hygiene by the Regimental Medical Officer would also be done by this tried and true method. Here we saw a white coated army Captain addressing us in the proper (i.e. army) way of using the latrines (one did not use the toilet here!):

"For the purposes of instruction" the RMO would say in a medical but military monotone "going to the latrine is done by numbers…" He would forgo the usual initial demonstration but would begin the countdown thus:

"On the command '1', enter the cubical;

'2' undo the belt (military, black, man for the use of);

'3' drop the trousers (Battle Dress Khaki);

'4' drop the shorts (tighty whities to us);

'5' defecate and/or urinate (not our terms);

'6' paper up – paper down (horrid slippery stuff!);

'7' Flush toilet or cover your load in the field;

'8' dress shorts and trousers (or dress if female);

'9' exit the cubicle; and

'10' wash hands.

Wow! Luckily my mother was never in the military as I would never have become potty trained as I couldn't count past three at that stage and I would never have got out of our bathroom.

Our weird day dream came to a sudden and very abrupt end by the arrival of Sargent Major Strang, our CSM and Bozo.

"Oh No!" came a quiet and very much subdued cry of despair from someone in our ranks. 'The Strangler' as we had named our CSM was never a joy to meet. He seemed to play the angry and belligerent NCO to the point of stereotype. He was an unhappy man at most times and only seemed to get a little ray of sunshine in his life by torturing the rank and file, namely D – Company.

"Platoon!" came that harsh but familiar voice. Somewhat like gravel being ground up in a cement mixer. We all quickly stood at attention and assumed the army rigid comatose position.

"Right Dress!" he ordered and we went to the process of opening the ranks, and dressing by the right. It looked like WO2 Strang was about to give us one of his infamous inspections. Bozo quickly made himself scarce by walking around to our rear. 'The Strangler' started along the first rank and looked up and down at each man; his squinty eyes searching for some deficiency. A hair out of place here, a whisker not fully removed by the early morning cold shave or some crease in the uniform that was not perfectly straight. Finally, he came to Louey. Now Louey was a great guy. Always happy and the 'life' of any party. He had all of the best characteristics of the Italians which his hard-working, immigrant family had passed on. Nothing much phased Louey in his open innocence.

'The Strangler' came up to Louey and looked down at his sloppy uniform, his bluish chin which no amount of shaving could erase and his Labrador-like grin.

'The Stanger' lifted up his pace stick and gave Louey a firm jab into his copious belly which was now hanging over his belt. "Do you know what is on the end of my stick, soldier?" he growled.

"No Sargent Major." Louey replied innocently, looking down on the end of the stick which was still making an indentation in his copious belly.

"There's a piece of s**t on the end of this stick, soldier. S**t!" came the belligerent response.

Louey looked down again at the end of the stick then looked up with big, brown innocent eyes to a point past 'The Strangler's left shoulder. "Well it's not on my end, Sergeant Major" came the innocent reply. J.C. who was standing behind Louey tried unsuccessfully to stifle a guffaw.

Warrant Officer Strang, Class II had met many a Dozy Digger in his long and nasty career, but never someone like Louey. His face suddenly turned purple with rage and his fingers tightened around his pace stick sufficient to put finger prints into its brass fittings. Not wishing to show his feelings (too late!) nor strike an enlisted man, he did a precise about face and marched off fuming with rage. The rest of us tried very hard to stand in our rigid ranks without falling about in hysterics. Bozo look the path of least resistance and eye of his superior and quickly marched around the opposite flank to our front. The smirk on his face suggested that he too shared in Louey's innocence. Somehow, Bozo's drill lesson on About Face was not quite as planned but at least it now had a new application for anger management. One skirmish won by D-company!

By now, D–Company was beginning to be looked at askance by the rest of our socially-acceptable regiment. For a start, we were an out- company which was simply another term for outcast and secondly that very few of us were or were studying to be accountants; only Gomez had some tenuous claim to that pedigree. It also did not help that we actually were totally unmilitaristic when it came to some of the etiquette of regimental life. There had been more than one of us who had been bawled out by some junior Second Lieutenant for something or other. They were now seen as the real enemy of our nation, well at least within the confines of Stalag Bandicoot. There always seemed to be a great surfeit of such beings wandering about the camp during respectable daylight hours, say between ten in the morning and four in the afternoon with a two-hour break in the middle when they retreated to the Officers' Mess for refreshment.

They always looked smart and carried clipboards in their left had, arm extended straight down the seam of their immaculate left trouser leg, their right hand ready to snap to a salute in return to that given by some unfortunate enlisted man who they should run across. As they wandered around the camp along most of the camp's many pathways, which was a regular event. NCOs, being well-experienced in such matters avoided them like stepping on a banana sandwich but twice as quick. They practiced true military movement and quickly walked to their destination between the huts and across open spaces making sure that there was a good distance out of saluting range between them and the Second Looeys.

Being mostly recruits or at best less formal members of an 'out company' where we were on more casual terms with our only officer, our reaction in meeting a sartorial apparition wearing one shiny pip and carrying a clipboard was to take one hand out of our pocket, give a casual wave and a cheerful "Gidday mate!" This did not go down well at all.

The next day, 'The Strangler' got his revenge. After falling out of bed to the dulcet sounds of our Reveille bugler and staggering out of our hut in greatcoat and boots for the usual muster, we were shocked to see 'The Strangler' standing at attention in full uniform. Bozo had had some inkling as to what was going to happen and had made himself scare.

"Snap to it!" be bawled as we tumbled out of the hut. Once lined up in some sort of bagman-like three ranks, he continued.

"Right! Back here in two minutes in PT gear. Move!"

Another new and horrible version of greatcoats – having dressed in one uniform, albeit sleep wear, greatcoats and boots, we now had to change into another. Our PT or Physical Training uniform consisted of white T-shirt, shorts, socks and sandshoes. Although it was still summer, at six in the morning at Bandicoot Hills, the temperature was as cold as charity in a workhouse.

Having fallen in, WO2 Strang marched us down to the parade ground across grass still crisp with morning frost. "Left, right, left, right…bring them arms up…left right, left, right…heads up! That includes you Private Puzzoso, you Dozy Digger!

We had an hour of this early morning Siberian torture. I looked across at Louey whilst attempting to do push-ups on my fingers as ordered by The Strangler, a thin layer of new frost was forming on his back. Time seemed to pass like a wet weekend in the nation's capital but eventually we were ordered back into three ranks. Bozo had conveniently shown up near the end of training and had taken command from WO2 Strang who had marched off with a grin on his face. Skirmish Two lost to the army.

It always seemed to me to be uncharacteristic of a fighting force to march in PT gear. It would only be worse if we had to march in underwear. We had passed several other groups walking back to their lines with towels over their greatcoats and boots wet with dew and grins on their faces. They knew and we suspected that our late turn at the showers would mean that all of the hot water would now be used and we would have to settle for cold showers and shave. Further punishment for losing the skirmish with 'The Strangler!'

After a cold and certainly not an invigorating shower and rough shave, we individually wandered back to our lines to hear Bozo wandering down the corridors shouting that the uniform for the day was 'Greens with full webbing, no pack'. Something to speculate on whilst having yet another bland breakfast of gelatinous eggs, white bread toast and lemon spread.

Promptly at eight, Bozo called us all out: "Fall in! Three ranks! Greens, webbing rifle... and don't forget ya' bolts... that means you Shipley and Puzzoso!"

Back on the road with our green fatigues, equally green but faded webbing with ammo pouches and our rifles (with bolts now hidden in our top pocket).

"We are off to tha' range, you lucky fellows!" said a smiling Bozo who pointed to our trucks standing a little way up the road, Wheels Jones leaning on the tailgate of The Relic.

# Chapter Seven: Operation Hostile Takeover

Our training went on with few periods of real excitement. One event unfortunately added to D-Company's Bad Boy image when Louey was paraded in front of the entire regiment and charged an amount of ten pounds for innocently selling grenade pins to the troops. This little item was simply a round ring similar in size and construction to that used on curtain rails. It was found to be very useful for attaching one's mug to belt loops when marched to meals.

The Second-in-Command of the socially-responsible regiment had been tipped off to Louey's little earner at two shillings a ring, by some toady in another company who had not thought of it himself.

"It is an offence both civil and military to remove produce from the range…" and so on read Major Grimes, the regimental 2IC. It was delivered in the same tone as Chief Financial Officer Grimes would have read out the latest financial statement at his last Board Meeting. Louey in all of his innocence was rather unimpressed and always had the concept that his family's adopted country was one of opportunity. It was a lot of money and he certainly had not sold the one hundred rings to cover the cost of this fine; next camp he would bring a suitcase full of his Nonno's Grappa to make up for this loss.

The other exciting exercise, if one could use the word 'excitement' for an accountant's concept of military tactics, consisted of a simulated attack on an imaginary enemy position up a long, sloping hill. The method of attack was yet another unimaginative military manoeuvre which superiors had gleaned from some WW2 training manual. This technique was tried and tested, well, from at least the seventeenth century, and was known colloquially as 'up the guts with bags of smoke.' This was easy to put in practice by the younger officers who had little imagination other than how to carry a clipboard and salute at the same time. The enemy would be located, and at some ungodly hour before dawn, following a snatched breakfast of cold meat sandwiches, and the attacking troops at platoon strength, would assemble on an imaginary line, called with some imagination the Start Line, ready to attack. Two machine guns would be sited on each flank to give covering fire and one would go with the troops in the middle of the line. Bayonets would be fixed and smoke grenade would be thrown just prior to the attack. Assuming that everything was well planned and conditions were favourable, on command 'Advance!' the line would walk up the hill firing as they went, until they swept over the enemy position. The enemy of course, it was assumed, would be taken completely by surprise and would throw up their hands in surrender. The attack was always made with a ratio of three of us to every one of the enemy. In past battles, such as those at Austerlitz and Waterloo, this tactic involved tens of thousands of troops who advanced into each other and plenty of smoke was provided by their muskets.

During our infamous advance against a totally fictitious enemy, the morning was cold and windy and the Start Line was not well defined, as one of the lanterns had blown out. Moreover, 2Lt Biscuit had difficulty in finding his platoon in the dark and some of the men had forgotten their bayonets. When the sun finally appeared through the trees and the attack commenced, we found that the smoke from the two small smoke grenades, both a brilliant orange, was blown in the wrong direction back down the hill and into our faces. Keeping a straight line and straight faces as we advanced up the slope across very exposed grasslands was difficult. We felt rather naked in a military sense. This would not have been another San Juan Hill but an outright slaughter had there been even a single section of ten men dug in on top of the hill with a single machine gun. We arrived on top of the bare hill and milled around in a leaderless gaggle as Biscuit Junior was still panting behind us somewhere in the smoke.

Having survived the Battle of the Orange Smoke, we were marched back down the hill like nursery rhyme of the Grand Old Duke of York:

> *The Grand old Duke of York he had ten thousand men*
>
> *He marched them up to the top of the hill*
>
> *And he marched them down again.*
>
> *When they were up, they were up*
>
> *And when they were down, they were down*
>
> *And when they were only halfway up*
>
> *They were neither up nor down.*

We were waylaid as we were approaching our lines and hopefully a short break with the usual morning tea of stale cake and strong brew, by Biscuit Senior and the rest of D-Company. Diverted to the shade of a large fig tree we were happy to find a Tables FS with the usual urn of strong black tea, metal bowls of sugar and powdered milk... and of course the large cubes of stale sponge cake with white icing which defied even the strongest bite.

We were dismissed to get our morning 'char and cake' and then told to sit in a compact group in the shade, which at nine in the morning was still cold.

Biscuit Senior, his younger brother, Gomez and the third Lieutenant, whose name was Withers and apparently a competent officer and not an accountant; stood in a group in the sun getting some warmth. We were all called to Attention by WO2 Strang who had quietly appeared from his unobtrusive position from behind the tree. Sitting to attention was not the most comfortable position as any small school child would know in any outside assembly; legs folded and arms straight out onto the knees, fists clenched. Luckily, Biscuit Senior quietly ordered Sit Easy which meant that we should unclench the fists and sit up straight.

In a rare moment of military democracy akin to that other famous oxymoron 'military intelligence', he said that he had some good news for the Company.

Tomorrow he revealed, we would take part in Operation Hostile Takeover, the regiment's last major activity for the camp and a major Regimental Advance to Contact. Captain Biscuit was most excited about this revelation. We were tired and so it meant very little to us. The enemy, he said, were situated on the open plain west of us and the socially-responsible regiment was going to advance to a line of hills above the plain prior to sweeping down to annihilate the enemy. Of course, we all knew that there were no enemy at all and this would be simply an exercise of moving our grossly under-strength regiment of a little over two hundred men through the scrub and up more hills for a couple of days. We later found out from Bozo who had spoken to Gomez who had done this very same exercise several times before that the real objective of the Colonel and the HQ staff was a well-known vineyard down on the plain. In previous camps, this exercise had been given names such as Operation Active Audit, Operation Bold Balance Sheet and Operation Lethal Liability; names that only a group of military accounts could dream up at the extreme ends of their collective imaginations.

Biscuit Senior went on in rapturous tones how we would all have yet another early breakfast at 0500 and draw rations. This meant more cold meat and tomato sauce sandwiches, stale cubes of sponge cake and an orange as ration packs were unavailable. We would advance to our designated hill positions where we will hold the position and wait for the proposed regimental attack on the enemy now sitting innocently down on the plain. Resupply of water and hotbox dinners would be made at 1700 (i.e. five in the afternoon or for officers when the big hand of the watch was on 12 and the little one on 5) with further resupply the next day; no doubt the usually 4WD and trailer full of canteen corn flakes, powdered egg, white bread, cold meat sandwiches and more hot box meals that evening. Hot box meals were too bad! There was little an ex-army civilian cook could do to a beef and vegetable stew, tinned fruit and, if we were lucky, ice cream. Some of the old hands who were more experienced in army long-distance travel, travelled light and only took one dixie with them to eat their food. Thus, the night's hotbox meal usually consisted of beef stew mixed with ice cream and tinned fruit. A rather insalubrious fare but well received when hungry.

Dress for this exercise would naturally be combat gear with full pack and webbing. This meant that we would actually put our rifle bolts in our rifles, not forget our bayonets and have all of our combat accessories fully packed. Two full water bottles were essential, as Biscuit Junior had reminded us of his boring lecture on Water resupply in the Field, plus a spare set of clothing, underwear, toiletries, towel, eating utensils- including two dixies (except for the old hands), hats giggle – our bush hat, bed roll with its nightly inflatable-deflatable mattress tubes and thin blanket, basic pouches, insect repellent which didn't frighten any insects but smelt horrible and could melt plastic, spare socks (2 pair), boots and gaiters and boot polish to match.

To this list the old hands removed the useless 'bum pack' which hung from the webbing to carry the bedroll and stocked their basic pouches with jack rations in lieu of ammunition which was not required when attacking a fictitious enemy on an open plain. These jack rations would be muesli bars, small tins of fish, hard biscuits and packs of cheese. They not only gave the basic pouches that belligerent filled-with-ammo, look but were also useful in helping to fill its wearer. All of these artful military dodges were yet to be learnt by us new hands who took everything issued except our Battle Dress uniform and Hats KF.

Unfortunately, very early the next morning, the bugler beat the early morning dawn and got us all out of bed at 0400. Much too early for conscious thought. We went through a quick parade in our basic greens and ambled in ranks of three up to the dining hall for a quick breakfast on the go of a boiled egg, cold, unbuttered toast slabbed with lemon spread and drew our rations of cold meat and tomato sauce sandwiches (2 – troops for the indigestion of), hard tack cake and an orange which in true military style also was equipped with its own penicillin supply.

Within half an hour we were back on the road in front of our huts, fully kitted up and ready to go. Tubes of camouflage cream were handed around so that we could blend more easily into the natural surroundings. These tubes were made by a well-known cosmetics company, the contents of which consisted of some water-proof waxy substance having a similar composition to lipstick, except that the artificial colours were in basic black, dark brown and jungle green. There was a little humour as men smeared their buddies with a uniform jungle green followed by some artistic zig zags of black and brown. Only the whites of the eyes now shone out from green, brown and blackened faces and we hoped that in any real war that the enemy had never heard of the famous command about 'not shooting until you see the whites of their eyes.'

We all felt a little jaded at such an early morning but, as we marched up to the main road with our rifles in our depleted platoons, we at least looked like soldiers. Here were our many lines of trucks which would take us deeper into the vast Army Training Reserve and to our individual platoon Start Lines for the beginning of the fearsome Operation Hostile Takeover.

Second Lieutenant Biscuit, our Platoon Commander, had replaced his clipboard with a bulky-looking map case and was busily looking at his compass whilst wondering what all of the numbers meant. Our trucks were the last two in the long line of trucks pulled over on the side of the main road and we were ordered by Bozo to take the last one. Off we went to defend the country (and its vineyard) from invasion.

Half an hour later, along may dusty roads, the fine brown dust of which, only added to the sticky camouflaged faces in the rear of the truck, we arrived at our allotted Start Line. Debussing from our trucks and forming into an uncoherent gaggle around Bozo. Biscuit Junior explained that we were to be on the extreme Left Flank of the Advance. The rest of D-company would be off to our right and the other three companies off further still. Our platoon, like all the others would be advancing in Arrowhead formation with one section up forward in the middle and the other two sections on each flank. The right-hand section was responsible for maintaining contact with the Left Flank section of the next platoon and so on. In this ordered manner, the entire regiment would advance through the wooded hillsides in quiet stealth; or so the theory maintained.

Zero Hour came, a little later than the anticipated 0600 hours due to our brave leader searching for his map case which he had left in the truck. This being retrieved, he blew on a whistle which suggested that we should move off. Nice touch! Another hangover from WW1 tactics.

Off we went. One up and two back as the platoon pushed into the dense scrub. Out on the far-left wing of the arrow, there was little for me to see. Certainly, no camouflaged enemy waiting with an AK47 ready to take us all down. We moved slowly, rifle pointing out from waist level moving with the eyes as we scanned the scrub all around. Occasionally, I would look over to J.C. who was the next man off to my right. He was stumbling over various tree roots and seemed to be 'off with the fairies'. I hoped that he was keeping an eye on the next man to our right. I did not feel at all confident in using J.C. as a marker. I had bad thoughts of the two of us wandering well off the designated direction well away from the rest of the platoon.

We kept together, during our advance to our objective. I would be reassured by seeing Luigi further past J.C. looking serious, keeping low to the ground and looking everywhere, including up into the trees as his Nonno had done in the forests of Italy in the 1940's. On through the 'open woodland' – well that was what Biscuit Junior had described the country in his briefing the day before. No one had mentioned the tangle of low scrub, brambles, nettles, fallen logs and bandicoot holes which did not show up on Biscuit's military survey map (1950 as amended).

The day also got hotter as the sun rose higher in the sky. And hotter. And hotter. There was a brief halt at 1200 hours as the silent signal came down the line to drop where we stood. A wave downwards of the hand and we all dropped to a kneeling position. Drop! one ta' thee! Another signal. Non-military but rather universal as a hand going up to the mouth and an exaggerated movement of the jaw. Eat! Ta' three!

I sat down and looked across at J.C. whose head just showed above a small pile of brambles. He was taking a long pull at his water bottle. Oh well! Time for lunch. Out came the very non-military paper bag containing its salubrious packed contents. Cut Lunch Commandos, the Regulars called us with good humour. I now knew the full truth of the matter and unwrapped my cold meat and tomato sauce sandwiches. When did this menu ever start? Who was the military genius in the Army Catering

Corps who thought up this concoction? No, I couldn't blame it on the Regs; they would have insisted on the paper bag being jungle green to match the rest of our outfit. Another weird vision of troops crawling around in the jungle looking for their lunch bags which had blended into the environment. No! Only civy cooks brought in off the streets and paid a minimal wage and with minimal supplies would come up with cold, processed meat splattered liberally with tomato sauce! Well, at least it was food. I had some doubts, however, about the large cube of sponge cake with its bullet-proof white icing. Perhaps this had been an old recipe from an earlier age when the defending troops were forced to throw any heavy item down from the battlements onto the enemy below. The peel of my orange had a few spots of the blue mould which I recognised from my old Biology class as genus *Penicillium.* Perhaps this was a new trend in the cash-strapped C.M.F. for DIY antibiotics, I thought as I pulled away the peel and was delighted to find the fruit relatively juicy.

Up ta' thee! Came another silent signal with J.C. off to my right standing up and looking rather bewildered at such a short lunch and probably getting over its components. I shoved the paper wrapping into one of my trousers' copious leg pockets and continued my forward motion with 'continual eye search' looking for an enemy which we all knew did not exist.

This continued up hill and down dale, as the expression went. It would have been more appropriate to say through thorny scrub and over fallen logs. Finally, the scrub began to clear as did the open woodland of Biscuit's faithful map (1950 as amended). Now we found ourselves moving up a long and broad slope with the trees giving way to bare ground and the occasional bush. No more brambles and logs! Only small boulders over which to stumble as we kept our eyes peeled for the ever-non-existent enemy.

The sun was getting very close to the blue wall of mountains of the Great Dividing Range in the far distance when the slope flattened out and we reached the summit of the hill. By now, our arrowhead had become somewhat narrow and more of a misshaped garden trowel as the platoon had come nearer to the top of the hill.

Biscuit called a halt and so we all sat down. He ran around to each section waving his arms and pointing here and there where each pair of men should form their own personal defensive position. The sighting of the section's machine gun was the main priority and the rest of us in pairs would form a defensive perimeter around the sides of the hill between each of the three guns. Some of us were told to move a little way up the hill to give defence in depth. Having been allocated our defensive position, Biscuit ordered that we were to dig in, to complete our defensive position. Each of us carried a 'tools entrench', a very practical device consisting of a short-handled folding spade. Unfortunately, even such an efficient tool could not make the slightest dent in the rock-hard ground of our rocky hill. Realising that we were unable to dig trenches of WW1 variety, Biscuit amended his order to 'make shell scrapes'. These were simply a shallow scraping away of the topsoil to theoretically protect the prone body from horizontal-flying shrapnel. In this ground, two or three centimetres were all that could be ground out of the soil. Not much protection. 'Make sangers' came the second amendment. This meant to add a small pile of rocks around the downhill side of the 'shell scrape'. This we did, very much like small boys building toy forts for our toy soldiers. Not much protection either but that was the best we could do. Common sense rather than some great knowledge of military tactics suggested that any enemy worth his salt would simply remove the entire top of the hill with artillery of mortars regardless of our amended defences. Well, we had at least stopped for the afternoon and we were to wait until the sun went down ensuring that the enemy did not mount a dusk attack. We were happy to be staying in one position and our hotbox dinners would be here soon to combat the attack of the colder night air.

2Lt Biscuit now wandered around his defensive perimeter and had yet again re-sited his machine guns and the rest of the outer riflemen further down the hill. And then later further up the hill. The Grand Old Duke of York would have approved but we thought that this constant change in position was just another version of Greatcoats. Greatcoats on, Greatcoats off. For any young officer, positioning men around a hill in a defensive position was a constant problem; having them too far down the hill meant a large and perhaps indefensible perimeter; having them too far up the hill gave a small and defendable perimeter but an ideal small target for enemy mortars and artillery. Finally, Biscuit settled for a compromise as the number of small shell scrapes and piles of stones was beginning to make our little hill look like a Neolithic archaeological dig.

1700 hours came and went. So did 1800 hours and the Sun was rapidly disappearing below the mountains to the west but there was no 4WD and trailer appearing to our east. Biscuit wandered down to near where J.C. and I were piling stones in an artistic but military manner.

"Where the devil are they?" Biscuit mused aloud to himself. Bozo had also come down to see if he could help his Lieutenant as he was getting hungry. Biscuit pulled out his wrinkled survey map (1950 as amended) for the tenth time and tapped a round cluster of contour lines.

"We are here, so where are they? He muttered aloud, turning to his sergeant."

Bozo had been looking at a small pinpoint of light moving down a hill further to our north and across a narrow valley.

"Excuse me, sir" he said with all of the politeness and servility that he could reluctantly muster. "Do you think that those lights on the opposite hill might be them?"

Biscuit looked up sharply and followed Bozo's extended arm.

"Nonsense!' he said with the arrogance that only a Second Lieutenant armed with a map could exclaim. "They should be here! On this hill, look!" he handed the map to Bozo for his lowly opinion.

Bozo took the map and then looked around at the surrounding hills in the fading light. He turned the map around through $180^0$ and looked at the map and the hills again.

"With all due respect, sir" Bozo was now at the upper level of his good manners and servility, "I think that we may be on the wrong hill."

Biscuit snatched the map back. It had now been orientated so that north on the map roughly faced north on the land. Biscuit looked at it. Then looked again. He raised his head and looked across the valley at the other prominent hill and the very tiny light of a vehicle's headlights now disappearing down its slope.

"um..ah..um" came his quiet little boy response. "Get the men ready to move out!" came the Platoon Commander's voice as he quickly stuffed the even more wrinkled map (1950 not amended enough) back into its plastic map case.

"Sir, may I suggest that we harbour here for the night, sir. We can cross the valley at first light and pick up the next resupply at breakfast." Bozo replied in a grovelling tone that would have made any Middle Eastern carpet-seller proud. "It'll be dark soon and I don't like the look of the slopes into that valley."

Biscuit thought for a while, walked around in a small circle pretending to survey this part of his well-planned defensive position and then reluctantly agreed.

Assuming that our non-existing enemy would be more interested in attacking our equally non-existent defensive position on the opposite hill, Bozo took some initiative and went around the platoon and told us to get our shelters up and get ready to turn in. There would be no water resupply tonight and we would have to wait until tomorrow.

So, at first light next morning, having spent a very uncomfortable night sleeping on our army air mattresses which like the Duke of York's campaign went up and then quickly down again, we struck camp and followed Biscuit and Bozo down the hill, across the rather soggy valley and up to our new defensive position. We had just time enough to dig shell scrapes twice again when our long-awaited breakfast arrived. Wheels Jones arrived with the 4WD and trailer and, after reporting to our harassed commander, came over and gave Bozo a quiet but colourful serve about not being here the night before.

"It was horrible!" Bozo gave a mock whine," it was the most dangerous thing in the army which caused our delay; a Second Lieutenant with a map and compass!"

Fighting fit after breakfast, we settled down in Biscuit's defensive position in depth (Mark II) and waited our allotted time for the imaginary enemy who was never expected to show up. Meanwhile, Headquarters Staff and the Colonel had successfully overrun the vineyard down on the plain and had liberated several crates of Cabernet Sauvignon,

Chardonnay, Shiraz and Sémillon. Operation Hostile Takeover was considered a great success!

## Chapter Eight: If You Can't Beat them…

The annual camp had finally come to an end and the tired troops of D-Company threw their gear into the back of the trucks and themselves after it. It was a long drive back to the nation's capital and this time there was no travelling beer supply. We were generally too tired to care anyway; at least we had staged a successful escape from Stalag Bandicoot!

We had money in our pocket thanks to the Regimental Paymaster who issued us with appropriate and named brown envelopes from one hand whilst clutching a nasty-looking OMC in the other. No problems! It was all tax-free and as I was still receiving holiday pay from the Education Department, I felt rather satisfied.

Those of us new to the game also had learned some valuable lessons in defending the country from Army Camp Bandicoot. These included: how to avoid officers by skulking between huts on the way to showers; how to avoid saluting by carrying an armful of empty boxes when walking the camp; how to get a hot shower by being the last on guard duty and stoking the boilers; how hide our rifle bolts where no NCO could find them; and how stand asleep on parade whilst standing to attention. I had also found that I was a good shot with the rifle

There were also some valuable lessons gleaned from either the older hands or by bitter experience. These included: never volunteer unless one could gain a little something extra; if it isn't bolted down and is easy to carry, then take it; always carry extra jack rations in one's ammunition pouch; carry an extra water bottle in one's pack, giving three water bottles all up; bring your own alpine-type sleeping bag for warmth; don't waste time carrying the army air mattress as it won't stay up so use a child's airbed instead; if ration packs are used, collect all the FRED spoons possible as they are an attractive item back home; and learn to travel light by leaving the useless bum packs behind.

We also learned that army tactics in this regiment at least, went back to WWI and beyond and that one could not fully rely on the outdated training manuals which advocated the use of roadside hedges for cover and telling the time by the village clock. I had a real problem with some of the training and felt that if there really was an active enemy at Camp Bandicoot it was the conservative senior officers who did not know any better. The young Second Lieutenants where a danger too, and in a real shooting war, one could get very badly killed following the appearance of one of these apparitions. At least some of them survived and became First Lieutenants and Captains who had some sort of an idea about what they were doing. The most valuable lesson was to find a good NCO, especially an old Sergeant or Warrant Officer who had had some real military experience. These veterans did not talk much about their former lives; few returned soldiers did. At least they had some good ideas about living with the army and combating the real enemy, HQ staff.

Our annual camp over and back in the nation's capital, we recessed for the rest of the school holidays to resume the same old training in February. A few more recruits joined to escape the draft except for two who were returned National Servicemen who had done their two years in the regular army and now joined the C.M.F. They were great guys who tolerated our amateur ways and helped to put some additional realism into our training which continued to follow the WW2 training pamphlets issued by HQ. They would have a quiet laugh and gently suggest that hiding behind hedgerows was not going to stop a burst of AK47 fire and that village clocks did not really exist in Vietnam. Gomez and Bozo as our command group thought that all of this was good value and could only improve the unit.

Unfortunately, by October that year, I received a transfer back to Sydney. I would regret leaving my school as it was a good one, well run and with great students. D-Company was also a good social institution that had given me some military skills and a wariness of the archaic practices of the larger regiment as well as a feeling of depression about the military effectiveness of the C.M.F. Most of the guys in D-Company and even in our socially-acceptable regiment, tried hard to do the right thing and prepare for the unlikely event of the defence of our country, but the conservatism at the top, the poor equipment and out-dated tactics put a cloud of depression over our training. The last thing in the world that I needed was to permanently parade with the main body of the socially-acceptable regiment back in Sydney, so I reluctantly sent in my resignation from the C.M.F. I was lucky in so much as I had the freedom to do this. Having been indefinitely deferred from National Service, and as I was a volunteer, I was free to leave at any time.

At the end of the school term, I said my farewells to my school colleagues and my friends at D-Company and left the nation's capital with a heavy heart. I also felt guilty in some respect; I had joined as a protest and to be trained to defend my country. It had made no effect on the feral rent-a-crowd groups who still paraded the streets occasionally and now the newspapers were also echoing their negative opinion about our National Servicemen who were trying to uphold the county's honour in what had become an uncertain and very nasty war. My training would be almost useless in the defence of the country, especially as there were few hedgerows in Sydney and without an accountancy degree, I was never going to make it further in the socially acceptable regiment.

I was determined, then, to put my military career behind me and get on with the business of teaching and starting a part-time university degree as suggested very strongly by my superiors in the Education Department. My new school was a tough one which would require some additional efforts in the classroom and some caution with an indifferent administration. Luckily, I found that the students were similar in character to many of my childhood friends coming from a similar background to mine. I was soon adopted by the tough set at the school which ensured my protection from harm. The administration was totally incompetent and could not care less who I was. My university courses were long, usually at night with the course going for seven years minimum.

Fate is a remarkable concept. As a very young seventeen-year-old student teacher, I had entertained one of my college Education lecturers with my view that fate was predestined and that we would live out our lives accordingly. Puerile nonsense perhaps but my life seemed to be a succession of rapid, unexpected changes, mostly for the better. A divine predestination perhaps?

Fate stepped in again when I picked up the local community newspaper one chilly autumn and saw on the front cover a large photograph of a young, rather apprehensive Second Lieutenant clutching a handset in one hand and a rifle in the other. Next to him, with the radio on his back lay his Radio

Operator, rifle at the ready and looking equally apprehensive; whether it was due to the urgency of the military exercise or the inexperienced, map-board-toting young officer next to him. Reading the article, I found that the pair of soldiers was a C.M.F. promotion in one of the city's major parks. 'Join the Officer Training Unit and Make a Real Difference' was the banner below the photograph.

"Perhaps this is where I should be," I thought. I could make a real difference as an officer, and certainly could do better than Biscuit and his ilk. Besides, I would assume that the training of an officer, even in the C.M.F. would be much superior to that in the socially-acceptable regiment. I rang the telephone number given in the article and got onto a bored-sounding individual from Army Recruiting. I mumbled my new wisdom about the Officer Training Unit and was put onto another extension. There the equally-bored individual explained that it was true that they were looking for a new intake for this unit that would start in the second half of the year; a few months hence. My name and particulars were taken and there was a spark of interest when I told them my old Army Number and that I had already served two years as a private soldier.

"The papers will be sent to you, Mr Shipley, the interested voice now said. Perhaps they were paid per head of recruits! I hung up and wondered if I had made the right decision or yet another snap judgement which might lead me into trouble. I had already had a minor skirmish with the C.M.F and had retreated.

Several weeks later, I received an official letter stating that I was to report to the 21 Field Ambulance Depot for an Army Medical and find enclosed the appropriate medical forms (in triplicate). This looked a lot more professional than my first Army Medical by a civilian doctor and perhaps I would not this time have to wander through a crowded shopping mall carrying 500 millilitres of my precious amber fluid. Never make assumptions!

I was lucky, the university was having yet another holiday and that night was free. The depot of this august medical institution was not far from my home and so I was easily able to arrive on time for the 7pm (sorry 1900 hours) appointment.

I parked my car on the street and walked through the unmanned gates into the large hall, passing several green-painted ambulances with their large red crosses on white backgrounds. I wondered whether or not bandages and other surgical equipment was also pained green.

A bored orderly wandered over as I entered and asked what I wanted. I told him about the letter.

"Oh, you're for the Doc, are ya'" he casually replied "Sit over there!" he pointed to a long bench next to the opposite wall. The large hall was empty, badly lit, draughty and quite cold. Perhaps this could be converted into a makeshift hospital as required but it could equally double as a morgue tonight.

After about half an hour, a door opened at the end of the hall and a figure framed by the light called for me to come in. Doctors, whether civilian or military obviously did not receive training in Medical School in punctuality and there always seemed to be a long wait in any surgery. I understood how it worked in civilian practice, as doctors were always stretched for time with a constant stream of patients. Here in this dim and draughty hall with only the orderly and myself, the delay seemed another version of the military approach to time.

I imagined a standard Army Doctor as a white coated army Captain (with a stethoscope over left shoulder). This person had the rank of Captain to be sure and the badges of the Army Medical Corps on his lapels but the white coat and stethoscope were absent and he was much older than I had expected. He seemed to be rather in a hurry and so told me to sit down whilst he fumbled with the bundles of papers in front of him; my completed medical forms (in triplicate).

He stood up and asked me to take off my jumper and shirt. It seemed to be even colder in his office than outside in the hall. We went through the usual examination including the application of a sub-zero temperate stethoscope which he had retrieved from a desk drawer. I did not ask if it was refrigerated. Everything being normal; heart, lungs, two legs, two arms, he wrote these particulars down on my forms then told me to look at the eye chart on the back wall and read the acceptable second-bottom line.

**A T R O P I N E** it read in very large letters. One would have to be very vision-impaired not to miss these letters. Moreover, Atropine was a well-known medication in the treatment of nerve gas and was often mentioned at medical lectures in camp along with other impossible treatments such as how to survive a nuclear blast by wearing a gas cape and carrying a shovel.

As I was not stupid as well as blind, I read out this qualifying list of letters individually. Perhaps one would be failed if one simply spoke out the full word atropine; a knowledge of nerve agent antidote could suggest some sort of subversive knowledge.

Finally, it came down to the usual request for a sample of urine. This was almost a military historical institution and my imagination wandered somewhat. I knew from my new studies at the university in chemistry, that the original source of the element phosphorus had come from a urine sample donated by a person who luckily had a medical problem and excreted excess phosphorus salts from his body. The story about the accidental discovery of this element, which I often recounted to enraptured teenagers in my class, involved the random experiment of the famous alchemist, Hennig Brand in the mid-seventeenth century. He was, like many of his contemporaries trying to find the 'philosopher's stone', that magical substance which could turn lead into gold. As humans were God's creation, surely human material such as urine would be a good resource to analyse. Apparently, Brand was into distilling solutions and so had collected a large amount of urine from one of his servants. I now knew how the poor fellow felt!

The distilling urine had been left by Brand who had suddenly remembered that it was still going on in his basement laboratory. "Ach der liber! Der urine!" he may have said; well at least that is what I told my students. Running down into the darkened basement, he found that the glass vessel had boiled dry but was now glowing with a crust of fine powder on its inside walls. Brand had discovered phosphorus. The military connect here, was that until relatively recently, match boxes containing a strip of red phosphorus on their sides, and were sourced in Sweden by the army. Here, urine was obtained in large quantities, over some time I hoped, from their soldiers. My imagination wandered even further and I saw visions of battalions of Swedish soldiers being lined up to provide specimens as I was now being summoned to do.

"Å nej! Inga fler urindonationer![4]" The Good Soldier Sven would have exclaimed.

The doctor handed me a 250-millilitre beaker; about the size of a decent army mug. "Would you mind passing a specimen, please?" he asked and pointed to a screen in the corner of the room. Going behind the screen, I dropped my trousers and tried to pass a specimen of urine. And tried. And tried again. No luck. Unlike the Good Soldier Sven, I was not forthcoming with the specimen. Dressing, I came from behind the screen and sheepishly informed the good doctor that my bladder was empty, having made the big mistake of going before I arrived.

The doctor sighed and took the empty beaker from my hand. He had seen it all before and looked at me over his glasses.

"Look! There's a pub up on the street corner. Go and have a drink to get you going and then come back here." He said with a tired expression in his voice.

A great idea, I thought, so I thanked him for his advice and walked as fast as I could out past the bored orderly and into the warmer air of the street.

---

[4] "Oh no! Not more urine donations!"

There was indeed a pub at the corner and it was full of the usual crowd. I elbowed my way to the bar and ordered a pint of beer. This should be enough, I though. Although perhaps a second beer would be also in order.

After my two quick and unsociable beers, I walked down the hill back to the Field Hospital unit, not as fast and steady as I had walked up the hill. I never really had much capacity for beer. Back inside the doctor's office and behind the screen with my trousers around my ankles, I looked at the small 250 millilitre beaker which was now rapidly filling with my bodily fluid. Herr Brand and the Swedish Army would have been most impressed. Stopping at the 250 level was going to be a problem.

Luckily, I maintained some sort of bladder control and gave the doctor a very full beaker of urine. He muttered something and dipped some test-papers into the fluid. "Sugar levels, OK" he mumbled and stamped my papers with a big red stamp: APPROVED. A quick thank you and off to the latrine at the other end of the hall. What a relief!

No time was being wasted by the non-medical part of the army administration, for a week later I received another letter requesting my presence at the prestigious Victoria Barracks on the fringes of the city's central business district. When it was built in 1841, it was no doubt on the edge of the Colony's habitation, but now it had been surrounded by suburbia. It was a large complex contained within huge sandstone walls and would have had all of the prestige and power of the British Army at that time.

This summons was for a written examination to confirm (or not) my suitability to be trained as an officer in the nations C.M.F. There would also be a short interview with a military panel following the examination. A mere formality, I had hoped. My year's study of psychology suggested that this written examination would be some form of performance examination with all of the usual questions of mathematical sequences (easy), three-dimensional construction puzzles (harder) and odd questions about organisational and political terms (difficult).

On the day appointed, I arrived at the rather impressive sandstone arch and gate and was stopped by a Regular army guard. I told him my business and he gave me an understanding look as if to say "Poor Bastard!" but replied with a courteous and professional direction.

"Parking down to the left, Sir and you'll be wanting H Block over there." He motioned with an extended arm.

I thanked him and drove my car through the impressive archway and over to the Visitors' Parking Lot. This was not a large space as the army apparently discouraged too many visitors into their barracks/fortress. Nearby was a much larger car parking lot but each bay of white paint on black asphalt contained its own specific allocation in military abbreviations yet to be deciphered by mere civilians such as ADC-CGS, ATC, DGPERS, GOC, 2ICCC, OIC, SIGINT, VD & S and other such exotic terms, all of which really meant NO PARKING to anyone else.

I found my way into H Block and followed some beautifully-polished signs which said' This Way' which led me to a medium-sized hall with small tables and chairs arranged in school student examination formation. A small crowd of other men, occupying the rear half of the parade of desks, looking bored were counting the number of tiles on the wall or watching the large, ornate clock high up on the wood-panelled front wall.

"Sit anywhere." Came a quite mumble from an elderly officer sitting at a desk in front of the room under the ornate clock. I found a seat not too far into the formation and started counting the tiles on one of the side walls.

Eventually, as the hour hand of the big ornate clock got to twelve noon, the elderly officer got up and closed the door to the hall. No late arrivals here! In other armies they would have probably been shot.

The elderly officer carefully moved along the aisles and placed a thin booklet which was our examination paper on each of the desks in front of its waiting candidate. Bored with counting tiles, I had looked about me and found that in a hall which had desks for about two hundred, only had desks occupied by twenty-three of us. So much for the great recruiting drive.

"You may start now!" said the elderly officer who had again retired to his front desk.

As expected, the examination paper had the usual performance questions, but these, like the faded yellow paper upon which they were printed, seemed to be from another age.

"You buy twelve oranges for three pence, three farthing each. How much change should you receive if you proffered a guinea?" was a typical mathematical question. I expected that these examination papers had been here since the construction of the Barracks in 1841.

Luckily, having come up through the old system of money, weights and measures and distances, I knew that a farthing was a quarter of a penny and that twelve pennies made a shilling and that a guinea (another amount before my time) was twenty-one shillings. A bit of calculation meant that the oranges cost a total of forty-five pence or three shillings and nine pence so my change out of a guinea would be seventeen shillings and three pence. I wondered if there were any questions on future pages as to the correct sequence of loading a musket or how many horses where needed to pull a nine-pounder field piece.

Most of the questions were diagrams requiring the candidate to order them in sequence or determine which one was the odd one out. Relatively easy and some of the political questions required some general knowledge of the country's political system and how it functioned (well, for most of the time). Luckily, from my time in the nation's capital, I knew who the current Prime Minister was, his political party and the supposed function of such government agencies as the Department of Administrative Administration. I felt sorry for some of the other candidates who looked as though they had just left school and were hoping to escape the draft.

This trial over, we were all herded off to another cold and draughty hallway where we had to wait our turn for our interview. My companions in this military machinery seemed to be a good, but subdued bunch who had little idea of how the wheels of Military Administration (another oxymoron?) operated. Eventually it was my turn and I was ushered into another wood-panelled room by an elderly sergeant.

"Be seated, Mr...ahh...Shipley" an officer with the red tabs of a full Colonel said in a friendly tone. I sat and looked at the four officers sitting on the other side of the oaken table. There was a Lieutenant-

Colonel who had some unidentified lapel badge but a red infantry lanyard around his left shoulder, Major of the Medical Corp and another Major whose cap sitting on the desk bore the badge of the Army Psych Corp. All bases seemed to be cover. Two very senior offices, one probably the Commanding Officer of the unit and his immediate superior as well as one senior doctor and a psychologist.

The usual questions which I had anticipated were asked:

"What sports did I like?" came the Lt Col. "Team games such as football and cricket" I lied. I did like these games but had no aptitude for them. At school which encouraged these games, I tended to be chosen last for the team and was generally flattened on the football field. Later I went on to be a good climber, caver and skier all solo activities.

"What was your relationship with your mother?" ask Major Shrink. An interesting question. I had studied all about the Oedipus Complex in First Year Psychology the previous year but I felt like saying the obvious that I was her son. I resisted the temptation and mumbled something like we had a good, mother-son relationship and that she was good to me. Very bland.

A few other routine questions came, especially about my reason for joining and whether I thought that I had leadership qualities. To the first question I very much told the truth about needing to be prepared if our county was invaded (little chance) and to the second I proudly boasted that, as a school teacher, I had to muster leadership qualities to teach a large group of homicidal teenagers. This all went down well and there was a general nodding of heads and smiles all around. The interview was over and I was free to go and would be notified in due course.

Due course arrived on a Tuesday morning just as I was rushing off to school. I had been accepted as an Officer Cadet in Sydney Command's Officer Training Unit (SCOTU). Back into uniform. If I couldn't beat them last time, at least now I would join them and try to make a difference!

# Chapter Nine: White Tape

Another letter of summons! This time addressed to '6553360 Officer Cadet T. Shipley'. At last! I was a number again and I realised that once branded, one was always part of the herd. This was my old number from the socially-accepable regiment. The Army, like elephants, obviously never forget!

This official piece of literature congratulated me again for being accepted into the C.M.F.'s elite Officer Training Unit (Sydney Command). I was to report on a date provided, which luckily was a Tuesday night and so free of university lectures. Then I would be inducted. This made me somewhat apprehensive as I had survived the First-Year student induction at the university which consisted of the freshers being covered in multi-coloured flour and then sprayed with water to form a psychedelic paste. They would be then thrown into the university's ornamental duck pond. As a part-time student, attending only after four in the afternoon, I luckily escaped such puerile activities. Perhaps the army version would have jungle green-coloured flour instead!

Again, I drove through the gate of the prestigious sandstone walls following a very short interrogation by the Regular guarding the said archway from hostile takeovers.

"Where are you going?" the Reg asked?

"To the Officer Training Unit, C.M.F" I proudly stated, "I'm one of the new Cadets!"

"Thank you, Sir. Go straight ahead, you will need Block H." the sentry said in a monotone and I knew from previous army experience as a private that in his mind he spelt 'Sir' as 'Cur'!

Back again in the parking lot of Block H with its adjoining parking bays of many acronyms; there should have been a rather large parking bay labelled POSH – PARKING for OFFICER STUDENTS HERE. I was ushered into the medium-sized hall again but this time the formation had changed to, auditorium, troops for the use of, with seats arranged in rows sans desks. Eventually all assembled found a seat somewhere near the back. This was immediately changed in true greatcoat manner as we were all requested to move down to the front. This request came as a stern but relatively polite order from a rather evil-looking Warrant Officer Class 1 who now stood at attention just in front of the first row.

"Welcome to SCOTU!" he said without a change in his stern face. "I am Warrant Officer the unit's equivalent to Regimental Sergeant Major." The several rows of campaign and long service ribbons on his left breast and the Combat Infantry badge on his right backed up the authority of the nation's coat of arms on his left sleeve. His face had all of the characteristics of a weathered grey granite rock face carved out by a very long and active career, probably not far from past front lines.

"Sit easy, gentlemen!" he said in his gravel-coated voice. "The Colonel will be here shortly. Don't smoke."

Those reaching for their cigarettes very quickly replaced their hands by their sides or on their laps. No one was going to argue with our new ersatz RSM whose nametag below his combat clasp read 'WO1 Grant'.

A few minutes later, the Lieutenant -Colonel whom I had seen at my interview walked in, took off his hat and gloves and stood at the front of the low stage which took up the front of the medium-sized hall.

WO1 Grant, also hatless, snapped to a rigid stance of attention and said in a firm but quiet voice "Our new Courses, Sah!" A smart left turn and WO1 Grant quickly walked off into the wings of the stage.

"Good evening, Gentlemen." Our new Colonel said in a confident and commanding voice, " Welcome to Sydney Command's Officer Training Unit. My name is Lieutenant-Colonel Jaeger, the Chief Instructor (CI) and head of this unit."

Colonel Jaeger was a big man, standing well over six feet and was about middle age. He lacked all of the ribbons of the RSM but did sport the single green and yellow of the Efficiency Decoration (ED) which was a mark of his long service in the C.M.F.

"As you can imagine from our selection process, we only want the best men for the job" he continued " We will train you hard and most of your free time in your civilian lives will probably be taken up with military matters; either here or in the field."

"What free time?" I thought.

Colonel Jaeger went on to explain the purpose of SCOTU and his personal views of how officers in the C.M.F. should be trained. There was not going to be any clipboard-carrying chinless wonders graduating from SCOTU! Colonel Jaeger made a big impression on me and from the looks of awe on some of the faces of the younger members of our group, on most of the others as well. Finishing his short but very inspiring talk, Colonel Jaeger handed over to a stocky-looking captain who wore the uniform of a well-known Regular Army combat regiment.

"Greetings, Gents!" he said in a firm, no-nonsense voice accompanied by a grin which could be considered friendly or sardonic depending upon what was being said. "I'm the adjutant and Rockwell is my name. I'm the guy who makes sure that you are all trained in accordance with the high standards and traditions of the Army. His bar of more recent campaign medals and the Combat Infantry badge suggested that these standards were going to be astronomically high.

The introduction to the induction process continued without (thankfully) the usual bluster and waffle which I had previously experienced in such formal meetings within the army. We had been already divided up into three courses we were told and the lists of names for each course were read out. I found that I was in number 24 Course, the others being 23 and 25. Each Course came with a captain as senior instructor (SI), an administrative officer, two other lieutenants as instructors, a sergeant and a warrant officer class 2 as course sergeant major. Later we found out that there was a considerable number of personnel in the headquarters staff which consisted of a two more lieutenants and a good number of warrant officers class 2. As we had about sixty new recruits, the ratio of instructors to cadets worked out at about three cadets per instructor; a rather concentrated teaching ratio!

The main formalities over, WO1 Grant instructed us to "Listen up!" in a voice that was low but had the power to reduce buildings to rubble, and read out the new meeting rooms for each course. "Move now, gentlemen, please." This polite turn of phrase was delivered in the same low but powerful voice and no one, not even the Colonel himself would have delayed his move for a split second. We all bundled out of the medium-sized hall into the corridor of Block H and looked for our new destinations. There were obvious signs sticking out from three doors at the further end of the corridor labelled with the three numbers of each of the courses. I walked smartly (the only other choice was marching) down the corridor and went into the second room which was labelled 24. More chairs in formation, but this time they had an accompanying table. The group of our instructors stood expectedly in a cluster on the low front stage. We quickly took our seats, this time in the first few rows.

The Captain. Our new senior instructor introduced himself as Bill Soames and explained the basic philosophy of the unit. As we were to become officers, one had to develop respect for the soldiers and each other. This unit was not like any formal regiment he explained. Most of the training would be done at the course level and there would be only a few instances such as major camps and some exercises where the courses would combine. All aspects of an officer's life would be taught, from the basic skills of the infantryman to the etiquette of the formal Dining In. And in all things, we were expected to excel! There would be times of formal army procedures and times of more casual, group activity but we were expected to be the best.

He then introduced his staff who would be our teachers (army, for the troops of). His lieutenants were First Lieutenant Gareth Jones and Second Lieutenant James Fairweather. I noted with despair that 2Lt Fairweather wore the uniform of my former socially-acceptable regiment. Perhaps he had been attached to SCOTU because he had lost his clipboard or was not contemplating doing accountancy. In fact later on, we found him to be quite an agreeable young officer who was studying philosophy at the university. His academic leanings earned him the nickname of The Scholar or just Schols. First Lieutenant Jones was more outgoing, stocky and darker in complexion and often added pseudo-Welsh terms such as 'boyo' to end his sentences so naturally he was called Taffy Jones. Our Captain was rarely called anything other than Captain Soames or Sir but as we got to know him as a good chap and eventually a good friend. He earned the affectionate nickname of Soapy.

In time they all proved to be good officers, although Schols at times became introspective and often wondered about his role in teaching death and destruction to fellow human beings and reasoned that even an enemy set to invade the country had a soul. Taffy had no problem with such scruples and tended to recall his ancestor's love of killing the English on the mountainous borders of Wales. In time, there developed a bond of mutual respect and some degree of friendship with our instructors.

Our warrant officers (class 2) were both veterans of the Korean War and had had considerable service both in the Regular army and in the C.M.F. WO2 Richard Caruthers, our CSM, was a very senior state public servant and his assistant CSM, WO2 Reg Dale, a retired builder in civilian life. Both men soon became mentors rather than tormentors and good friends. Chris McCrery was our young sergeant who always seemed to have a smile on his face but was a tough customer when it came to drill and field craft. Never-the-less he was a friendly, approachable type and enjoyed a drink on occasions. He got on well with Taffy Jones and we all imagined that, in another era that they would not be past plotting some secret Celtic rebellion against the English of the colony we now defended. Due to the respect we had for their experience and tough good nature, we could not think of any nicknames for our two Warrant Officers but Sergeant McCrery was referred to in good humour as Scary McCrery or simply Scary.

Our introductions over, Captain Soames looked at his watch for the hundredth time and said "Right! Gentlemen, if you will follow me, we will get you the necessary kit." And he walked out the door. Stage Left. We all got up and, in a gaggle, wandered out into the corridor and followed our new leader. Back again to the medium-sized hall which had been cleared of chairs and now had several long rows of Tables FS – those ubiquitous long wooden, collapsible benches that were used for everything from eating food to surgical operations in the field. Behind the tables stood soldiers from one of the C.M.F supply depots who were now happy to dispense this bounty because of the additional pay they would receive for the extra duty.

There was the usual assortment of military gear which the fully-equipped soldier was expected to have and to maintain. Hats KF, battle dress khaki and beret, boots black, combat uniform Green (2 pair) and so on. There was also a pile of small, white tape folded over so that they could be threaded onto our shirt epaulettes. These were to be our badges of rank as officer cadets, much the same as navy midshipmen wore white tabs on their collars. Webbing with its basic pouches and ridiculous bum pack as well as our main pack were still of WW2 vintage. Even the elite Officer Training Unit did not rate the new, light-weight gear being used in Vietnam!

Once all of these items had been ticked off by the stores clerks and signed for by unsuspecting cadets who were now completely bewildered about the nature and use of the new-found bounty, we were told to take it all to our cars and then to parade in front of Block H. At this current stage of our training, to parad' meant to stand in some noisy huddle, except for myself and one or two others who also had had prior service who knew the meaning of the term but preferred to join in with our new ex-civilian friends.

With the new members of 24 Course, we were marched down, if one can call an amble a march, the bitumen road to a long, wooden hut nestled in the corner of the huge sandstone walls of the barracks. It was neatly painted as were the rocks which lined the pathway up to its steps. A small, hand-painted sign at the start of the pathway read Cadets' Mess. Things were looking even brighter. We were fallen out – a quaint army term for go anywhere but stay here! -whilst Sergeant McCrery opened the door and bade us all to enter. The inside of the hut contained many small tables with chairs, some bright mats on the floor and the walls were decorated with a number of flags, many of which bore numbers. No doubt these were the flags of previous courses. At the end of the hut was a door and a small bar. Things were looking up.

We entered and found our chairs not knowing exactly what the protocol was going to be. Captain Soames and the Colonel walked in and removed their hats.

"Well, gentlemen!" the Colonel said" this will be the last time that we shall enter here with you uninvited! This precinct is for cadets only. Officers, including myself must be invited to attend. Gives you a chance to bitch about your officers, huh?" he said in a jovial mood.

From the rear door, which was the storeroom for the bar, several white-coated orderlies, no doubt borrowed from the Supply Depot on extra pay, emerged with trays of food and jugs of beer were put onto the bar along with trays of glasses.

"The drinks are on the unit, this time gentlemen. Enjoy this welcome to SCOTU. Next time we meet, we will all have to earn our drinks."

With his introduction to our very own mess over, we settled down to a quiet social evening and some rare fraternisation with our commander and his staff. The army now was looking like it really had some potential. The defence of the country would have to wait…. well at least until next parade evening.

## Chapter Ten: The Democratic Course

The army administration seemed to be working overtime. Only a few days after my rather gratifying induction, I received yet another letter in its dull khaki envelope. It was my Joining Order to attend my basic training camp with SCOTU. I read it and suddenly was hit by a very unpleasant bout of déjà vu! I read the offending line again…and again just to make sure that I had read it correctly. I had hoped that there had been a mistake! No! The letter clearly stated in that military language used by army administrators and police reports:

"You are to make your own way and at your own expense by car, public transport or other vehicle thereof to Army Camp Bandicoot Hills, 4077 Bandicoot Road, Bandicoot Hills."

"Oh No!" I gasped. "Stalag Bandicoot!" I had thought that such a prestige unit as SCOTU would have caught up with modern times and found somewhere closer to the times. When I had told my family of my army experiences in the nation's capital and of my camp at Stalag Bandicoot, my father had had a great laugh. He too had once attended the very same camp as a young Light Horse Trooper in the

Militia in the 1930's. We had compared experiences and they were identical, right down to the coal-fired hot water furnaces and the dodge of taking last roster during guard duty. I guess that in an ordered world there was little need to change.

"All appropriate clothing and equipment (as issued) was to be packed in accordance with Army Regulations and Military Orders (AR & MO)" whatever they were! So, I collected all of my prized kit and caboodle and everything except my battle dress, beret, belt, webbing and Hats KF were stuffed unceremoniously into my new jungle green canvas kit bag. As I was Full Bottle. Or as the Americans would say savvy to the conditions at Stalag Bandicoot, especially now in a very cold winter, I packed some useful jack items. These went into a separate bag and included my alpine sleeping bag, a child's blow up air mattress, several pairs of woollen football socks, a Balaclava head covering (Khaki), two pillow cases and a flannel sheet doubled over and stitched to form an inner sleeping bag (Thanks Mum!), an extra towel, an iron and a hot water bottle. I also included a bottle of civilian-brand insect repellent as a potential replacement for the revolting army brand which came in a jungle green bottle and which would dissolve plastic and repel fellow soldiers but not the hardy species of mosquitoes which inhabited the environs of Stalag Bandicoot. Several tins of black boot polish and a good cleaning rag went in a separate cloth bag obtained for that purpose; the army liked its spit and polish! I also packed a good supply of jack rations including a box of muesli bars, small tins of tuna, small tins of fruit, glucose lollies, a packet of cream biscuits and two of my previously purloined FRED army spoon/tin openers.

I loaded up my small car the night before, leaving out my battledress, beret, black belt, boots and gaiters; the last three items having been spat and polished to my best standard. Polishing one's boots, gaiters and belt was a nightly exercise in my former military life and I wonder what verbal venom my new colleagues, who had not had the experience of former army life, would receive from the sun-cracked lips of RSM Grant at our first inspection of their dull, unpolished boots, gaiters and belt.

I had also taken precautions and had had my hair cut - very short. This was the sixties! Male hair length rivalled that of the female of the species and even conservative male school teachers sported hair to the collar – those that still had hair! I had gone into my local barber and asked for an army haircut. The old barber who had no hair himself and probably served in WW2 if not WW1 almost cried at this request. Very short back and sides (with top included) a-la-army, had not been requested in his shop since the early fifties. Whilst humming an old, forgotten light air, he deftly cut my hair which seemed to fall in great swathes onto the floor. He delighted in his work. During this systematic shearing, I recalled the alternative consequences. I had remembered my first Basic Camp with D-Company which, situated in the University of the Nation's Capital, had rather relaxed standards of the military haircut. At our first parade, the Strangler had sidled up to J.C. and, putting his nose about two centimetres from that of his hapless victim had quietly said in a soft voice:

"Am I hurting you, son?"

"No, Sergeant-Major." The innocent J.C. replied.

The Strangler's voice then went to its usual high volume as he continued:

"Well, I should be! I'm standing on ya' bloody hair!" he yelled and sent J.C. off immediately to a local civilian barber who had been brought into Stalag Bandicoot expressly for the purpose of cropping the hair of luckless recruits. I had a vision of my current barber but with scissors and cutthroat razor in hand and an evil gleam in his eye just waiting for customers to report as ordered.

I drove my car through the unwelcoming but familiar gates of Army Camp Bandicoot Hill. Nothing had changed except that there was no guard on the gate and a small red and white sign with an arrow proclaimed SCOTU was down the only road leading into the camp and past a gaggle of men standing around the Guard House. The car park was eventually found, well out of the main complex and beyond the parade ground in a large, overgrown paddock. Several cars were already parked in the long grass including a low, Lotus Elan sports car which had the grass almost to its windows. Only the fact that it was a bright red colour prevented it from being totally assimilated into the long grass. Its owner still might have some difficulty in locating his vehicle at the end of the camp. Later, I found out that it belonged to Terry

McDowell, a very keen member of number 23 Course. The joke soon spread that his was the only car in the carpark which could be run over by a snake. And the grass grew even higher.

I hitched my heavy kit back and webbing over my shoulder and picked up my smaller bag and walked back to the gaggle of men standing around the Guard House. These were going to be my colleagues of 23, 24 and 25 Courses SCOTU. A very unmilitary looking bunch. Most carried a variety of baggage with or without their kitbags. One tall, skinny beanpole of a fellow stood by a very large grey metal trunk which he somehow had dragged the long distance from the car park. This was Rick Worthington. A fellow member of 23 Course.

"What's tall and has a big grey trunk?" would be a popular question spoken in jest on occasions. No, it wasn't an elephant! It was Worthington, The Elephant Man! This was usually shortened simply to Elephant or even Wortho, but he was a good-natured type and often took the brunt of jocular criticism as he became the course's uncoordinated eccentric.

WO1 Grant suddenly appeared out of nowhere and ordered us to get into three ranks in a firm but rather respectful way, considering our respective positions. Warrant Officers all seem to have this talent of appearing suddenly out of nowhere; perhaps it was part of their training or simply just experience gained out of years of being able to disappear just as fast when a Second Lieutenant with a clipboard appeared. Whatever his earlier experiences, WO1 Grant seemed a man of diverse talents but yelling at the enlisted was not his style.

It took a while for the semi-civilian gaggle to form into three ranks and when it did so, there still was no resemblance to any military order. I looked around at my colleagues and saw a great variation in the army uniform, haircuts, baggage and general deportment. What a bunch of pseudo-soldiers! A few, like myself had obviously had previous indoctrination and wore their combat uniforms (as ordered) with some sort of order. Most, however had items which were going to be very shortly changed. Some Hats KF were unblocked, many belts, boots and gaiters still showed the dull glimmer of their original preserving wax and a few unfortunates had hair hanging down to their shoulders. The Strangler would have had apoplexy! Not here! WO1 Grant walked along the ranks and made some quiet comments to those who needed some attention. This would be given later that day by their Course Sergeants. Only the long haired were asked quietly to fall out and directed to the Guard House where the army barber waited with baited breath and razor sharpened. The other Warrant Officers and Sergeants appeared and stood down the road in three groups. WO1 Grant read out the names of each of the three courses and we were directed to pick up our baggage and re-form three ranks in front of our respective CSMs. The Elephant Man dragged his heavy trunk down the road with some effort.

Now in our respective courses with our own instructors, we were starting to feel like a cohesive unit. We were assigned our hut, appropriately Hut 24 and told to square away and sort ourselves out. This was done with the help of Sergeant, Scary McCreary, who went from room to room assisting each misfit to get fit and proper (his words). An hour later, back on parade with our CSM, WO2 Caruthers now, we had begun to resemble soldiers: Hats KF were blocked in an acceptable style; belts, boots and gaiters now were polished, and most uniforms had creases where they should be. I noticed that one new feature on the end of each hut was a large notice board. The CSM pointed this out ("Don't turn your head, son!") and explained that from now on, the daily routine of our training would be posted – daily. This being done, he handed over to Scary McCrery who then marched us down to one corner of the parade ground for some elementary drill practice – all by numbers, of course. Our new life in the army had started.

At lunch break, I was disappointed in finding that things had not changed; cold meat salad with lashings of white bread, army butter and lemon spread. At least there were some new bottles of Vegemite[5] on the tables. The army tea was just as strong with cordial in the side urns just as weak.

The next day we were introduced to a concept that was new to old hands such as myself who had suffered under the tongue-lashings of Drill Instructors. Each day we had a designated Duty Cade' who now had the responsibility of an ersatz

---

[5] A black, grease=like spread of yeast extract beloved by Australians and similar to the British Marmite, German Vitam-R, and Swiss Cenovis and almost unknown in cuisine-challenged America.

officer-of-the-day. It was his role to see that we all tumbled out for early morning PT (Physical Training for the as yet untortured) or sick parade for those who knew what was coming. Sick parade soon dispensed with as the genuine sick, injured and maimed reported directly to our Regimental Medical Officer (RMO), another captain armed with a stethoscope and of unsympathetic demeanour.

Now here was a problem for Number 24 Course! We were all very keen to become officers and being a Duty Cadet was a great way of finding out who had natural talents in this department. Some, who had prior experience with officers or who had watched sufficient John Wayne war movies soon developed a natural quiet leadership style. Others who had little experience, varied in their use of role models from the sadistic Sergeant Dagineau of the Foreign Legionnaire movie Beau Gest which was now playing, to some ineffective chinless wonder from some Carry On movie. In addition, we were still aware of the transient nature of such leadership, so it was not uncommon for some dissention to occur in the ranks when being marched and directed by some hapless Duty Cadet who was still unsure of how to give directions.

"Squad will turn to the left in threes, left turn!" said the Duty Cadet.

"Wait a minute!" came a voice from the ranks. "Aren't we going over there to the right?"

"Nonsense!" came another voice from the ranks. "We must keep on straight ahead."

"Let's put it to the vote!" came yet a third voice.

Soon the vox poluli degenerated into a series of alternative suggestions with the Duty Cadet trying to shout over the lot. Number 24 Course soon became known to all and sundry as the Democratic Course, not without some derision. I am not sure how the military decisions were made in the early days of the Democratic People's Liberation Army, but it soon became obvious that a consensus of opinion was not conducive to the giving of routine orders.

Soon we found that the members of 24 Course had more than its share of eccentrics, all thrown together for various reasons into the C.M.F. We soon became good friends and although the other two courses were like-wise situated and some good friends were also made in their ranks, there still was considerable friendly rivalry between each course.

Now, at the very beginning, we had decided to follow the long traditions of SCOTU's short establishment of some eight years and have a course flag. This was designed after long hours of democratic consensus in the Cadet's Mess with the details getting more bizarre with every round of drinks. Finally, the KISS principle was invoked to stop an in-house war within the army, and we all settled on the 24 Course flag being a golden crest on a bottle-green background. In keeping with our new-found democratic reputation, we had an ornate scroll added below the crest with the Latin motto 'Quot homines, tot sententiae' – 'many men, many minds'.

Indeed, when we got to know each other more closely, and there is nothing like an army Basic Training camp for getting to know your new friends, we found that we were a diverse mix of characters. All of 24 Course soon fitted together as a close band of brothers held together against the difficulties posed by the conditions in the C.M.F. and the media propaganda of the time. Those of us who had seen service before such as myself and the laconic 'Tommo' Thompson ex-National Service, knew that we were all lucky to be in SCOTU. Our Senior Instructor, Colonel 'Big John' Jaeger was an exceptional leader both in his civilian career as CEO of a national engineering company and here in the C.M.F.

His philosophy was that we should be best of the Weekend Warriors, maintain extremely high standards in all things military and civilian and become officers who would lead from the front with respect for our men and for any potential enemy we could one day face. He had his own opinion about army tactics which would have horrified my former tormentors in the socially-acceptable regiment. As a young Lieutenant stationed in India as an engineer building dams in the Himalayas, he had managed to get himself attached to a Gurkha regiment and had become a fervent disciple of their methods and tactics. None of this 'up the guts with bags of smoke' for Big John! We were civilians training to defend our city or country against a professional invading force. Stealth and fire and movement were his two major codes; stealth in and around an urban jungle and rapid fire and movement within any country environment. Indeed, his brand of the old Rifle Corp Light Company supportive fire was also unlike that practiced by other units of the C.M.F. and regular Army. Instead of one section group moving whilst another gave fire support, he trained us in a complex manoeuvre of several groups moving in different directions under covering fire with rapid change in fire support/movement groups at speed. This meant that we would advance rapidly under covering fire from a several changing positions. The theory behind this form of small-unit blitzkrieg was that an enemy would find it difficult to find a target confronted with several small groups moving quickly in different directions with support fire also advancing and coming from different vantage points. Of course, he hated having to defend open plains; this was for the Armoured Corps. He advocated keeping to the confines of city buildings and streets or in some high country with plenty of cover by rocks and trees. Unlike the arrogance of other units, he did not assume that we would have air superiority nor the backup of the US Cavalry if we got into a tight spot. His heroes were the great guerrilla leaders of previous wars such as: T.E. Lawrence (of Arabia); David Stirling, founder of the

British S.A.S. (that's the Special Air Service, not our Saturdays And Sundays C.M.F!) and even some from the other side such as Mao Zedong, Otto Skorzeny (Hitler's ultimate commando leader) and 'Che' Guevara from Cuba.

Colonel Jaeger had the radical opinion that if the country was suddenly invaded by a small, secretive but determined force and the C.M.F. was eventually activated, then we would probably have to steal ammunition and equipment from our local supply depots who were not noted for being generous to the C.M.F. In his vision, Colonel Jaeger imagined a deceptive invading force, most likely from a country which did not play cricket nor adhere to the Marquis of Queensbury Rules, suddenly showing up in a disguised freighter in Sydney Harbour on either a Wednesday afternoon when the Regular Army played sports or on a weekend when they would be on leave. This would have been considered Bad Form by the gentlemen of regiments such as the socially-acceptable regiment and other conservative units of the C.M.F who might have had the misfortune to be on duty on such a poor weekend.

Our other officers also came under Colonel Jaeger's leadership philosophy but, for the most part, lacked his dynamic understanding and rank to freely express it. Our NCO's accepted such ideas but most had had combat experience along more traditional lines and tended to follow their training as regulars.

Within the ranks of 24 Course, there were a great variety of ideas and personalities; many men, many minds. With the exception of our youngest member, we all had various reasons for being in the C.M.F. I wanted to get some better training if the implausible Domino Theory was correct as did others, but some were there simply as an interest, were curious or simply wanted to play soldier at a time when the country had committed itself to yet another war. Our youngest member, David Donaldson we affectionately called Dozy because as a nineteen-year old Arts student always seemed to want to sleep, was there to escape the draft.

Our oldest member was Heinrich Isaac Schwarzwälder-Hügelbewohner who was in his mid-thirties and who had escaped NAZI Germany and the Holocost as a young child with his parents. He was  known as Henry but we called him Hans because he still had a slight trace of a German accent and would pronounce all of his w's  like v's, and besides he was well-built and had blonde hair. Apparently his grandfather had been an officer in the First World War and Hans wanted to follow this tradition. As we were to get name patches for our combat uniforms, Hans had a big problem, namely his name! Whilst he was very proud of it and his German ancestry, he decided for purposes military to shorten his name. It was suggested that if he did not do this he would be the only member of SCOTU who would have to get a  bar[6] to his name patch. Accordingly, he initially decided to use a shortened version of his name as Schwartz but then on further contemplation thought this too Jewish so he anglicised it to Black. We were all disappointed in this surname switch from Schwarz, so we simply called him Hans which he accepted with grace. Many years later, as a non-so-young Lieutenant he switched back to Schwartz and joined the Israeli Army as his own personal protest.

---

[6] Recipients of military awards were given a bar to their award if it was awarded a second time. Our Assistant CSM, Reg Dale had been in the army for over thirty years and had a bar to his Long Service and Good Conduct Medal.

Another older character who got on famously with Hans was Ruban Rose. He was a free-wheeling type who had breezed in to the city a few years back to get work in his trade as a motor mechanic.

"Call me 'Roo'!" he had cheerfully said at his first meeting in our group. He had been a semi-professional hunter from a place called Bunyip Flats way out in the west of the State where the crows fly backwards to keep the dust out of their eyes. He loved weapons of all sorts and if it made a loud noise, all the better, although he had some doubts about our 7.62 mm SLR.

"Gimmey a good Winchester .243" he had once said when first issued with our rifle (and bolt to be well-hidden). "A solid 80-grain shell, not the city-fella's 100-grain, mind. A good well-placed 80-grainer knocked over a Roo far quicker than the 100-grain due to its higher velocity and increased shocking power. See?"

We all took his word for this but he proved to be an expert shot and the best in the unit. I pity any kangaroo if Roo ever went back to his previous occupation back in Bunyip Flats!

The third member of the old timers in 24 Course was Immanuel Ball. He was a friendly and innocent fellow who was also a Lay Preacher at his church. In the first few days of our meeting at Camp Bandicoot, he had raised concerns about some of the bad language issuing from the rest of us at stressful times. It seems that on entering army camps the world over, its members, no matter how innocent and naive soon found their collective use of language deteriorating to some lowest common verbal denominator. We accepted this and did try hard to reform but this earned Immanuel Ball the nickname of The Deacon.

Then there was my best friend Paul Sinclair. He was an irrepressible and hyperactive type who looked at all military training as something to be totally embraced and enjoyed. He was an agent in some import-export business and had spent most of his time travelling the world and had a great talent for getting on with people. He also liked a good wine occassionally (every day if possible!) and the story was told that during a wine-bottling at his company, he fell into the vat and it took three attempts to get him out; he had escaped during the first two attempts. Good at everything, including personal relationships, he later became our top cadet and as such was awarded the the sword of honour to lead our graduation parade at the end of the next year. Most of the others in all courses called me Ships which had been my sobriquet since my schooldays, but Pauli thought that as a potential leader should have a more militant name, so he stuck me with the title of The Commodore. This was O.K. by me. But it eventually died out, especially when some of the others modified the title to The Commode Door.

Under normal circumstances, the eccentrics of 24 Course, and there were the same types in the other two courses, would have given their instructors a difficult time and probably turned them to drink if they had not already been there as young soldiers. Our instructors were firm but fair and so we cooperated and generally tried our best. Even Dozy Donaldson started to shape up as a potential officer and carried his duties quietly but with a modicum of efficiency.

# Chapter Eleven: Extra Training Value

I once had a good friend, departed now unfortunately, who was a Colonel in the C.M.F. and took several tours to Vietnam, including several trips up the Mekong in small patrol boats. When things got tough and the bullets were flying, he would simply smile at his frightened troops and say "Extra training value".

Luckily, our training with SCOTU was not as dramatic but it was hard and long. Whilst the C.M.F. soldier was required to do the equivalent of thirty-three days full time training, we did over one hundred days in our six-month program. This included most Tuesday nights (one third of a day), our basic training and another woeful winter camp in the second year and two annual camps at the end of each year. All camps were held at our alma mater at Bandicoot but many weekends and whatever attached duties our beloved Senior Instructor could wrangle from Army HQ were held at a variety of places.

We were being trained for all of the arms and services operated by the C.M.F. This could mean appointment to the Infantry, Artillery, Armoured

Corps, Engineers or the Service Corps. Because of this, we often visited either for a day or two or as an extra camp, some of these other branches of the C.M.F. I liked going out on Sydney Harbour with the Water Transport part of the Corps of Engineers but my idea of applying for the unit later was dashed when I was told that I would have to have an engineering background. Bother! Wouldn't a degree in Geology count? No! Go and dig holes in the dirt with the Infantry.

So, we wandered into the Artillery who were still firing WW2 25 Pounder guns and today was to be a live-firing demonstration. Because of my science studies, I was given a radio, a map, compass and a pair of artillery binoculars and dumped about a mile from a target hill. My colleagues in the other three Courses were taken to a battery of six howitzers to learn how they were loaded, aimed and fired. I was the volunteer Forward Observer who would give directions to the target and adjust any fall of shot. I wasn't sure that only one mile was sufficient for the nine-mile snippers – as the artillery was called – and hoped that they knew their job. My mind wandered to a vision of fanatics like Roo or dreamy types like Dozy loading and aiming six guns in my direction.

Never-the-less, I did the mathematics required on the map and in calculating the distance and the amount of charge from a book of tables then radioed in my target information, hoping that it was not also my self-destruction. I had heard of war heroes who had called in artillery on their own positions as they were being overrun, but I was not in that category. I had been issued with a helmet, but that was not much protection against six 25 pounder, high explosive shells.

"Shoot!" I called over the microphone in a rather tremulous voice. A short wait and then the muffled sounds of six guns firing simultaneously (well almost!) in the rear. A very short wait and then the weird sound of the shells streaking overhead like some sort of express steam locomotive. I focussed by binoculars onto the large wooden targets sitting high up on the hill to my front.

The targets and the top part of the hill disappeared in a huge cloud of grey smoke with flashes of high explosive. Wow! What an awesome sight.

"Adjust?" came a little voice on the headset. "No need." I responded in a very unartillery manner "the target and the hill have gone!"

"But we need to adjust fire!" came the incredulous voice from the other end of the radio.

"Well, there's no target left!" I replied. This was not good enough for the purposes of the exercise...load ta' three, close breech, ta' three, shoot, ta. Three! So I had to work out some more figures for the rest of the hill still standing so that our artillery hosts could go on with further actions for the benefit of my colleagues who were oblivious to the destruction going on a few miles to their front. The demonstration shoot over, I was extracted – thankfully from the target area and returned to my curious friends.

"Give us tha' details, Sport!" asked Roo who fell into raptures as I describe the intimate details of how to remove a hill from the countryside.

A few months later, we again headed off for a weekend camp in the army's training area well west of Camp Bandicoot. This was simply going to be an exercise in reconnaissance and living in the field. For this latter purpose, our instructors packed a truck with tents including a big marquee. Several Tables FS and several large insulated cold boxes, called Eskys in Australia, with steaks, beer, wines and all of the older basic rations needed for an officer's field bivouac. This was going to be a great weekend. Three courses also piled into trucks and off we went to our area of operation.

Everything set up, we were broken up into several small reconnaissance (recce) patrols. My group under Dozy Donaldson as patrol leader, consisted of myself, Hans, Roo and the Deacon. We were to patrol some of the denser woodland several miles west of our camp. Major land features and any enemy activity was to be plotted on our map and we were to report back by 1700 hours. Unlike my previous regiment, the Colonel believed that there should be an active enemy in most of our patrols and for this he used the sergeants and lieutenants of the unit who were called directing staff. On this occasion, they were not active, but we weren't too sure. Colonel Jaeger liked to keep us all on our toes.

It was a good day and we reached all of our objectives and noted them with due care on our map. Our last hill feature was quite a distance from camp and Dozy had read the map upside down a couple of times until the rest of us showed him the error of his ways. The light was beginning to fade behind the long row of blue-coloured mountains to our west as we headed for home, smugly confident that we had done a good job and would impress all and sundry with our arrival. Off along the old 4WD track we went; in line but marking with the ease that Regular soldiers would call swanning along, rifles held at the trail position by our legs as we walked and talked. Very slack, but what a nice day?

Suddenly, as we came around one of the many bends in the road, we saw coming our way a patrol of NAZI Storm Troopers also in file and walking on the other side of the track. NAZI Storm Troopers!! What was going on? We all came to a shuddering stop like a bunch of rail carriages bumping together.

"Gosh!" muttered an incredulous Dozy who was leading us into some form of time warp.

"Bugger me!" said Roo.

"What the F**k!" blurted out the Deacon forgetting his New Testament teachings.

"Heiliger Strohsack![7]" (or words to that effect in German) from Hans who had lapsed into his boyhood German.

We all stood there with our mouths open and eyes wide open as well.

The NAZI patrol continued towards us, the faint light of the late afternoon Sun reflecting off their black, coal-scuttle helmets and their Schmeisser machine pistols.

"Seig Heil!" said their leader, giving us an open-palm, chest-high salute as they quietly passed, their heads down as though in some monastic chant.

We stood transfixed as they walked past, our eyes and heads following them down the track and our hearts somewhere up in our mouths.

"NAZIs" came our combined cry and we fled in a gaggling run along the track towards camp.

"NAZIs" we all yelled hysterically as we half stumbled and half fell through the first ring of tents into the firelight of a huge camp fire. The rest of our combined group, standing around this fire in

---

[7] 'Holy Smokes!"

various degrees of non-tactical relaxation, raised their cans of beer and chorused "Prost!" and then fell about laughing at our facial expressions and trembling lips "NAZIs!"

Bill Soames, our SI, finally gave us First Aid in the form of a can of beer and instructions to sit down, and put our heads between our legs and take a deep breath. This was standard army First Aid for anything from shortness of breath to nuclear attack.

Having taken our mandatory deep breath, Bill explained that there were really no NAZIs but rather a group of Regulars dressed in character for a television drama shoot about WW2 going on down the road. Their director had come into camp earlier that afternoon to warn our unit about the possibility of some battle sounds and uniformed troops in the vicinity. Of course, we were the last (or lost!) patrol into camp that evening and the Reg 'extras' had decided to go out and meet us just for laughs (they said). It took us a little time and a few more beers before we saw the funny side of this encounter. Hans was not happy and had to be restrained by another beer from fixing his bayonet and going after the Storm Troopers.

The next major function was another Commanding Officers Discretionary Period which meant that the Colonel had been able to wrangle some extra training over and above our due time. This was to be a two-week attachment to the Regular Army's Education Corp to do specialist training in teaching our future troops. It was called Methods of Instruction and was designed specifically for junior NCOs. As it happened, we had to qualify as corporals to go into our second year of training. So, proud of our two stripes and our white taped shoulders, we were bussed (in trucks, naturally) to the main Regular Army camp which was also on the western fringes of the city. Our accommodation was still in the lower order of accommodation, still being in long huts, but far more comfortable than Stalag Bandicoot. There were real sheets on good mattresses and the food in the Other Ranks (ORs) Mess was superior to anything I had experienced. Napoleon would have also been most impressed and his army would have marched a lot further on their stomach with such fare.

On day one of our course, we were marched into a rounded Nissen Hut and sat down at attention, a most unnatural mode of seating only performed in the military and some formal private primary schools.

"Sit easy, remove your hats!" said the old Sergeant who stood on the small stage in front of our class. He started the lesson.

"Right! We're here to show youse how to give appropriate instruction to ya' troops." The voice was hard, gravelling and far from the intellectual tones of staff at my university. I had had some misgivings about this course. After all! I was a professionally-trained teacher of several years' experience. What could old guys like this fat sergeant teach me about teaching?

"Right! I'll have two volunteers. You and you!" he said pointing to Dozy who had nodded off as usual at the command of sit easy. And Roo who was looking out of the window trying to find some piece of ordinance which he had not yet fired.

"This will be fun!" I thought.

There were two clean blackboards (painted army green naturally) standing on each side of the stage. The old fat sergeant handed his two new recruits a large sheet of paper which they had to show us had a good and accurate picture of Mickey Mouse drawn upon it. A beautiful copy – Walt Disney would be proud of the line drawing.

"Right!" the old fat Sergeant said. He seemed to start every sentence with that word, probably his way of grabbing attention to the hard of hearing – a common complaint amongst the lower ranks when there were orders being given. "'ere is a nice, simple little drawing for youse two young gentlemen to copy onto them blackboards (army green, naturally)"

"This WILL be fun!" I thought for the second time. Dozy had difficulty drawing breath and Roo was more used to drawing a bead on some luckless kangaroo. Off they started.

Roo was inscribing some image between that produced by some badly-trained cubist on drugs and a spider which had walked across a chalk box. What a shambles! A few laughs and pointed fingers from the audience who felt lucky that they had escaped being volunteered.

Meanwhile, over on Dozy's blackboard (army green naturally) a perfect image of Mickey Mouse was being drawn. Even Walt Disney could not have done better! Our mouths dropped open again. Wow! What talent he had. This was totally unexpected as Dozy had not been noted for his military skills or any other that we could discern. Both artists finished and put down their chalk. Roo looked at us with a sheepish grin as though he had just missed his target at five metres. Dozy had the broad grin of success on his face.

"Right!" said the old fat Sergeant yet again. "Ya see these tow drawins? One's 'orrible and the others a ripper! Right! This is wot we're gonna teach yer gentlemen to be like. The good one, not the scribble1 " Roo shrunk down a little in his regained seat.

"Right! Young Corporal, tell yer mates how yer did such a good drawin."

Dozy got back on the stage and shyly pointed at his great drawing.

"Well" he said shyly "the drawing was already on the board in pencil. All I had to do was follow the lines."

What a great idea! No one at Teachers' College ever taught us that and all of the drawing which I had seen in the classroom on black or green boards (I was proficient in both) were of a far lower standard than the one made by the untrained Dozy Digger.

This little Motivation Step introduction, for that was what the purpose of the exercise really had been, set the scene for two weeks of educational enlightenment for me. I had thought that my condensed and experimental two solid years at Teachers' College had been innovative and extremely functional, but this system of the Methods of Instruction team was something beyond that. In a short two weeks, the Education Corps team of NCOs and officers had us all become confident and skilled instructors on any topic, military and civilian. The final act was to have us each in turn come out in front of the assembled three courses and give an impromptu speech on a random topic drawn out of a hat. Even the Deacon, who was naturally shy and hesitant in his speech unless it was on some Biblical topic, stood up and gave an inspiring speech on the usefulness of desktop nametags. We now felt like we could take on any dull squad of bored soldiers.

The extra training was now over and we returned to our HQ at Victoria Barracks to get ready for our final examinations, both academic and practical. There were many army training manuals to study, most still going back a few years, drill of all sorts to be practiced and a final shoot at the Regular Army's firing range.

There a three-hour examination on Military Law as officers sometimes had to be judge, jury (the executioner phase went out in the 19th century) and mediator. We had two very large law manuals, each about the size of an old-fashioned telephone book and as it was an open book exam, the appropriate pages had long since been tagged with small paper squares.

For this exam, we had been marched with our two massive tomes, into the medium-sized hall at the Barracks which was yet again in desk-chair military formation. Questions on the paper often were rather cryptic and consisted of case-studies which required a Solomon-like judgement. One question read:

*"Private Bloggs of your Platoon is off duty. He goes into a local pub where a fight ensures and being a large, well-trained soldier, he inflicts great damage on the furnishings, bar and most of the patrons. Accosting the Publican's wife and stealing money from the till, he throws his Hats KF at the last man standing who has a*

*heart attack and dies. Bloggs also sets fire to the establishment upon leaving. What are you under Army Rules and Regulations able to charge Private Bloggs with when he resumes duty?*

Some of my colleagues thought very deeply upon this particular question and wrote out a long list of offenses ranging from Murder to general Mayhem, not to mention accosting the Publican's Good Lady. By their calculation Bloggs would probably not see the light of day outside of a Military Prison for at least a hundred years. There were places in our historic Barracks which were probably designed for just such an offense.

No! I reasoned; it would be up to the local Police to take Bloggs in. All I could do as his hapless Platoon Commander was to issue him with a Lost and Damages form and charge him for the loss of his Hats KF which was lost in the subsequent fire.

So much for Military Law. There was a long period of testing for our First Appointment as Second Lieutenants in the C.M.F. Finally, the results were posted on our Cadets noticeboard and we found that all of us had graduated: Pauli getting the sword of honour as our top cadet, Roo came second (probably because he spent all of his army pay on getting regular haircuts) and I came third due to my academic results and shooting prowess, only second to Roo's bullseye destruction. All the formalities over and a very extensive session in the Cadets' Mess where we felt it some sort of military honour to drink everything still left in the back storeroom. We had two days to locate our heads, polish everything that was leather or brass and get ready for our final Graduation Parade.

This was to be a very formal occasion. All of our relatives and friends had been invited that Saturday and the parade was to be in combat greens with bayonets fixed – except for Pauli who carried a sword out front. The parade was also to be on the hallowed Parade Ground of Victoria Barracks upon which the boots of many a British Regiment marched before handing it over to the Colonials. It was to be our version of the Guards at Buckingham Palace and so all of the Military hierarchy from the Colonel upwards would be there. And it rained!

It did not just rain, it poured. Cats, dogs and buckets could not describe the deluge that day. The Deacon was ominously chanting verbatim the Book of

Genesis (Chapters 6 to 9) about Noah, and the rest of us just looked forlornly out of the window at the solid sheet of water coming off the roof. Our guests where huddled opposite under the awnings of the 19th Century verandas and somewhere, also under shelter, was the army band who was striking up a series of lively marches. Handle's Water Music would have been more appropriate!

The Colonel burst into the room with his usual grin which he wore in the face of disaster.

"Well, boys!" he said in a loud and jolly voice. "What is to be? You go on to parade as you have been trained to do and damn the weather, or line up under the veranda outside to go through some arms drill?"

"On with the parade!" three Courses yelled loudly.

"God bless you boys" said the Colonel flushed of face." I'll enjoy it yonder with the General." He pointed vaguely out the window to a red-bannered set of chairs on the dry veranda opposite.

WO1 Grant came in beaming and then went around to every man and checked his full kit, uniform, shaven face (even Roo's shaven head) and said

"Well, its time. Line up in your designated three ranks outside and right dress. Don't let a little moisture dampen your spirits!"

"A little moisture!" I thought, looking out of the window. If the Deacon had his way, we would all be pitching in on the construction a large wooden vessel (troops, civilians and other life for the use of).

The band struck up the get ready chords of the quick march Our Director and off we went, Pauli leading. Into the sheet of water. Left, Right, Left, Right.

"Keep your eye on the man to right" – Roo in this case with a big red sash across his chest – we all thought. Watch where Pauli is going. The centre man in the front-rank whispering instructions to our very wet leader "more to the left, On!" Left, Right, Left, Right. Right Wheel. And so, it went on. Like a groom at his wedding, we just got on with full concentration in our marching and listening to Pauli's orders over the howling rain. The brown dye from our chin straps running down the sides of our faces. Our boots making maritime-sounding noises on the soaked turf, now several inches below water level. All the while the water poured down our

necks and to every inch of our bodies. And the band
played 'Waltzing Matilda".

# Chapter Twelve: Back to the Front

Well, we had all graduated without so much as a scratch. The last military tasks before we were unleashed on unsuspecting units of the C.M.F. was to be fitted out with our new supply of uniform. Once more for the last time, we had all been assembled in the medium-size hall for our last issue of kit. Like a bunch of schoolboys being issued our new team shorts (in school colours), we dutifully lined up whilst the supply boys proffered peaked caps (officers for the use of), several versions of epaulettes (hard and soft) and an additional supply of single, brass 'pips' – the shiny little button things which went onto the hard epaulettes to denote one's rank. Second lieutenants rated one of these precious items per shoulder. In time, and if we were lucky, they would advance along the shoulder like some reproducing caterpillar, firstly as two (first lieutenant) to then to three (captain). We were also given a chit and telephone number for the army's preferred tailor who would then personally fit us out for our dress blues uniform. This piece of sartorial discomfort consisted of a pair of dark blue, almost black, set of trousers with a strip down each side depending upon the unit to which one was posted; infantry for example had a solid red strip and the armoured corps as being descended from the cavalry had a yellow strip. The coat which went with the trousers was a throwback to the last century and was a very heavy, long-sleeved wool felt unit which buttoned right up to the chin with a row of very shiny brass buttons. At the top was a very stiff collar which went right under the chin. In any weather other than an Antarctic gale, this uniform was extremely hot as well as uncomfortable, but it was our only issue for the many lavish and high-class formal dinners which we were expecting in our future units now that we had reached officer class.

Most of us also went out and purchased some items of our own. The army-issue peaked caps, for example seemed much too stodgy, for want of a better word; somewhat like a new private schoolboy's hat which had come straight off the school shop shelf. There was not character in our peaked caps, they had a relatively hard upper section which made the entire cap look ridiculous. Far trendier for the newly-appointed young officer was the soft top peaked caps which looked very militant when worn at a jaunty angle (except when the CSM was around!). For our much-anticipated social life, we purchased the 'mess dress undress', also known as the 'ice cream jacket' because it resembled the short white, open jacket worn by soda jerks as seen in all of the popular American teenage films. This jacket actually looked smart with its brass buttons and fitted with brass unit label badges and pips on the soft epaulettes. Worn with the blues trousers, white shirt, bow tie and red cummerbund, one would cut quite a figure for the ladies. Of course, it would be only the poor officers below the rank of major who would wear these outfits to military dinners and balls; the senior officers would purchase the more elegant full-dress uniforms which were red in colour and carried, as appropriate, more shiny brass. A Sam Browne Belt was the final self-purchase to complete our new uniform. This was a broad brown belt with a shoulder strap going across the body and was worn by officers and warrant officers when on official duty such as Officer-of-the-day and other outdoor formal functions such as weddings and funerals (as a guest only!)

We had been given a large collection of forms (all in triplicate) to fill in before leaving SCOTU. One of them was an application to join our future Arm of

Service. We had now to decide where we would like to go as 'king of the kids' (or 'kids of the king' the old NCO's would say). I chose to return to the infantry as I knew how it worked and would be unencumbered with the heavy metal vehicles of the armoured corps or the guns of the artillery should ever a shooting war started and I would need to invoke my prepared escape route.

Pauli, Roo and I were eventually posted to separate battalions of the same (and only) infantry regiment housed in our State. The Roo soon found that his new troops could not stand the intensity and tactics of his introduced training, which would even make the Commandos or S.A.S. consider a civilian life, so he later resigned his commission and went to Africa to join the mercenary circuit then popular amongst local dictators.

Hans liked all things big and so joined the artillery and the Deacon went to the service corps in the hope that, like the Gideon society, he would be able to dispense copies of the New Testament to every soldier in the C.M.F. Dozy went the ordinance corps to supervise the packing, storage and even perhaps (on rare occasions) the distribution of ammunition.

We all wondered when the first explosion would occur and resolved not to go anywhere near his ordinance depot.

My view of the fate of Man once again came to pass and I was commissioned into yet another out-company of the State regiment. A-Company was, luckily a much better setup than my old D-Company in the nation's capital. It consisted of a relatively new two-story brick complex, double garage and broad parade ground all encircled by a high mesh fence topped with razor wire. The gates were open most of the time but closed at night except on Tuesdays which was parade night and then they were closed when the last officer staggered from the Mess reparked his car on the side of the road and finally found the gates.

I arrived early on Tuesday night, parked my little car and walked through the imposing double glass main doors.

"Evening, Sir!" said a smart-looking corporal at a desk just inside the door. "Officer Commanding's room just down the corridor." He continued as I was just about to ask. He was one of those NCO's blessed with second sight and knew what most officers wanted before it came into their head.

The door was open and so I knocked and entered.

"Tom Shipley, Second Lieutenant 6553360, reporting for duty" I announced giving the figure sitting behind the desk a smart salute.

The figure was a captain who looked up at me from under black beetle brows with small, wild-looking bloodshot eyes.

"Ummmh..huff..ah yes…Shipley," he replied in a fast-staccato voice. "From SCOTU, I believe." He rummaged around a great pile of disorderly papers and pulled out a small brown folder, obviously my file. "Ah….umph…huff…yes. Very impressive. Welcome to A-Company." He said in a monotone whilst I still stood rigidly to attention. "Go and see Warrant Officer Baumann in the next room. He has all of your duties arranged. Good evening."

As the formalities were over, I gave the dark Captain another crisp salute as my cap was still on, about faced and walked smartly out of the door and did an even smarter right turn. There had been little real welcome by the dark, red-eyed Captain commanding his desk and I had the vision of some lone figure on the walls of a desert fort being the last man standing who was determined to defend his little world at all costs. I wasn't even sure whether the Captain was sitting down or standing up as he seemed to be rather squat in his general appearance. Oh well, Napoleon was only five foot six inches tall.

At the second door, I now felt a little like Alice in Wonderland and wondered where I would be sent next. This time I removed my cap as I was obviously in the presence of a superior being at least in experience if not in rank. I knocked and went in. The figure sitting behind the well-ordered desk with its piles of papers in strict military formation was different in every respect from the OC.

He was an older man, probably in his late fifties with a deep, sun-tanned face bearing the wrinkles of experience on his brow framing his deep blue, penetrating eyes. A smile came to this comfortable face when he looked up.

"Mr Shipley, is it? Ah…. please sit down. I have been expecting you. Welcome to the regiment and Alpha Company." Now I felt welcomed at last. I'm Sergeant Major Bauman, the CSM and Regular

Army Cadre of this unit." He picked out yet another folder from the top of a pile of papers which again was obviously my file. I expect that the army's usual triplicate folder as at HQ which was in another suburb well down the railway track which ran just outside of the razor-wire fence at the rear of the compound.

"I see that you had previous service as a private soldier?" he continued.

"yes Sir…umm Sergeant Major." I corrected myself. One did not call Warrant Officers sir.

"Well that's good for you. Most young officers haven't a clue about what the average soldier thinks and so I suspect that you already know of a few dodges, huh?"

"Yes, Sergeant Major." I grinned. I was sure that WO2 Bauman knew many more dodges, looking at his chest full of campaign ribbons, his Long Service and Good Conduct ribbon and the Combat Infantry badge above his right pocket. He was still a Regular but had been posted to this C.M.F. as Regular Army Cadre staff, that is, a real soldier posted to such units to assist in their training. Or in other words, to keep us on the straight and narrow.

He pulled out a few papers from my file, inspected them closely then looked up.

"Well, for the time being, until you find your feet here you can be Assistant Training Officer under Lieutenant O'Halloran for a while and help him sort out the training here."

My previous dodgy training as a private filled in the missing pieces of this appointment. Lt. O'Halloran was probably not up to scratch, the training program was probably a shambles and for the time being, WO2 Bauman would be seeing what I was made of. Fine! He looked friendlier than most Warrant Officers I had met outside of SCOTU and the task at hand seemed easy enough for an experienced teacher who had had to develop his own training program for a school of over three hundred in his first year.

For the time being, I soon found that this was not as easy as I had imagined. Jimmy O'Halloran was an easy going and friendly guy but there was a suspicion that he had come from the shallow end of the gene pool when it came to all things military. Despite this, he had risen to the rank of First Lieutenant and had probably achieved his by doing his minimum duty and little else. His main claim to fame which he was immensely proud of was that he had finally, after two years hard trading acquired all of the army's training pamphlets and guide books which he kept in a small bookcase in the rather untidy training office. This, unfortunately was the sole reference for his style of training. He had quietly confided in me that everything... repeat everything... needed for training was here. I smiled to show interest in his great achievement and picked up the little grey book headed Tactics and opened it at random.

*"Prior to attacking the enemy in a frontal attack, apply a plentiful amount of smoke before emerging in force from behind the covering hedgerows"*

Oh no! Up the guts with bags of smoke and concealment by hedgerows! The bane of modern tactics and urban warfare! I was back in the conservatism of the C.M.F infantry.

So, my usefulness at Alpha Company was put on hold whilst Jimmy O'Halloran issue out-dated training manuals from his beloved collection to the sergeants and the other two officers who had real contact with the troops. My other two colleagues, both second lieutenants who had almost acquired the appropriate time to gain a second pip to their shoulders, were also friendly types; Jonny Burgess and Bill Connel seemed to be competent in their roles of Recruitment and Administration respectively and we all took turns in commanding the three platoons which the company should have had on establishment. In fact, we were greatly under strength and on parade, our three platoons consisted of a sergeant, corporal and about fifteen men. Platoons in name only, so training was usually carried out in bulk in company strength (ha!).

The lustre vanishing from my sole pip on my shoulder, I settled in to the usual Tuesday night training at A-Company and soon learned to fit in with its long-established pattern.

Our gallant captain was called William Willis, although I had heard a few of the men and at least three of our officers refer to him as The Gnome as he was often off with the fairies at HQ. He was rarely in attendance at our Company Headquarters as he often went to conferences at Regimental Headquarters further down the track towards the city. This actually meant that he was trying to become visible in front of the colonel and any other influential, person who could assist him in gaining his majority; his main military objective. Captain Willis usually huffed and puffed his way about the company when he was in attendance and had an eye for petty detail but not for the big picture of what was going on. It came as no surprise to me when I heard that he was an accountant.

So, the running of our company on Tuesday nights fell to its lieutenants with the able support of our four sergeants, at least two of whom knew something about the infantry. Tom Cutler was very good, mainly because he was former Regular Army but he chafed at having to train the men under Jimmy O'Halloran's instructions and outdated army manuals. His only problem was that he had little imagination and was very traditional in his own way. The other sergeant was a character in his own right and had enough imagination for all of the sergeants put together. This was Sergeant Neville Cholmondeley-Smythe, known to all as Nifty Nev.

Nifty was a mover and shaker in a rather quiet, low-key way. He had been born in the East End of London and had brought all of his parent's cockney ways with him when they immigrated some ten years earlier. Now, not all East-enders fit into the rather unfair stereotype of the barrow-pushing cockney; but Nifty did! If fact he seemed to want to play out such dodgy characteristics and in the main par, for the good of most. He was the man in the entire regiment who could get it for you at a good price and there was by no stretch of imagination to believe that he was a clerk in the Department of Customs. He was a good man to have in any army unit and especially in the C.M.F. as scroungers were often needed to get anything of value in our training.

A good example of this came later in the year when I was attached to an Armoured Corp unit during our annual training camp. They had shown incredible initiative and vision to ask our regiment to provide an infantry platoon which could act as enemy during their own training. Having an active enemy during full-time training was a hobby horse of mine and I had often aired my views on this subject in our rather rambunctious Sergeants/Officers Mess after training and after more than advisable number of Salty Dogs – the Company's deadly gin/grapefruit concoction taken in a glass rimmed with a crust of salt.

It may have been the subtle work of WO2 Bauman who had become something like the equivalent of the kindly military uncle mentor to me. He had appreciated that I wanted to take the troops to a practical level beyond that which the other officers had been prepared to do and had silently agreed with this point of view. Naturally, he had an extensive network of underground communications with the regiment and within the army in general. He was an old hand of great experience, having been an advisor to anti-communist hill tribes in South East Asia well before the Vietnam War had even started. As an efficient sergeant in the Regular Army, he had trained many aspiring soldiers who were now generals and others in power.

Captain Willis almost fell over himself backward, which would have easy for him, considering his short stature, when the word came down from the Colonel to get an enemy platoon together with me in command. I had found my calling at last and my war with the C.M.F. conservatives could now take on a practical dimension. SCOTU Colonel Jaeger's tactics were about to hit the Armoured Corp.

Nifty, who thankfully was to be my Platoon Sergeant, and I scratched together a full platoon of volunteers who wanted to get out of the usual boring camp training of drill, lectures, drill, pointless advances and drill. We were collected at our camp, as usual at Army Camp Bandicoot, the preferred and only camp available at the time, and driven in trucks to a new training ground over one hundred miles to our north in the Hunter Valley. The area consisted of several heavily-wooded and boulder-strewn hills overlooking a broad undulating plain of open grassland. In the midst of this plain was the main camp of a Mounted Infantry (MI) unit, our enemy.

Their CO was a good type and obviously wanted some realistic training for his Troopers who were carried around in Armoured Personnel Carriers or APCs. They had once been a Light Horse unit but had traded their horses in for things mechanical during WW2. My role would be to sit somewhere and be attacked by the APCS and, in true Custer and 7th Cavalry fashion, die like a man. In the meantime, to prepare for our imminent demise we were directed to a rather heavily-wooded copse of trees in which we could camp. This last comment was said almost with a smirk, because the gentlemen of the MI, sporting cavalry-yellow cravats and black berets were very comfortable in their camp of large marquees which covered everything from their personal lodgings with camp stretchers and blankets, mess tent, Quartermaster's Store, canteen, and even the latrines. The whole place was well-lit with camp lanterns and probably could be seen from space had anyone bothered looking.

We had what was on our backs and would sleep tonight as usual under 'tents half shelter' connected together to form open-ended and very drafty tents for two men. As usual, our army air mattresses would deflate in the middle of the night and the local ground was very cold and hard. The good news was that we could share their mess (if our boots were clean) and their latrine but to do this, we would have to cross a rather deep and nasty gulley between our camp and theirs.

Here Nifty's talents came in handy. After he had carried out a rather detailed and subversive reconnaissance of the Trooper's camp, he came running into our pitiful little harbour to tell me that, unlike most Infantry Units, the MI's had a second lieutenant (with clipboard) who was their Quartermaster. A target pigeon if he had ever seen one! Moreover, Nifty had found that their supplies also included some of the latest packs and new uniforms and so had spun him some pitiful tale about our badly fitting combat uniforms and WW2 equipment

"Hi, Guv." He said with breathless excitement, giving me his usual title of respect. "They 'ave a Quar'ermaster hoo is a righ' mark faw a bi' ov  ol tradin' like. 'E will swap one faw one faw for any ov our old malarkey!"

This was great news as many of the men and I had purchased ex-Vietnam packs and spare greens at our own expense and some of these looked like that had gone through 'second hand' several hands ago.

"Right!" I said, borrowing a decisive action word from my former training. "Get the men to sort out all of their crap gear – clothing, boots, gaiters, and definitely their packs and form them up in two ranks ready to raid the cavalry!"

Off we went. Down the gulley, up the gulley and across the open, grassy patch to the MI's nice, shiny stores tent. After a short introduction and an officer's version of Nifty's tall tale, their chinless wonder put down his clipboard and got his people into the store-keeper's business of issuing the bedraggled infantry with their new kit. Apart from the new Vietnam packs, we were also lucky in exchanging our WW2 boots and gaiters for the modern, ankle-fitting Boots General Purpose Boots GP). What a find and another successful infantry raid!

That operation was done on the QT according to Nifty and I assumed that it was not to be made known to the other officers of the MI. What came next was a major exercise demonstrating my views that the infantry could do anything. Thanks to Col. Jaeger's lectures about the versatility of the Legionnaires of the ancient Roman army.

This all came about because the MI boys had been doing some manoeuvres just out of camp as a forerunner to their main destruction of the enemy; us. They found out most dramatically that high-speed runs of their APCs across a plain with long grass could have some problems. After a good season of rain, the grass was now over three feet high but dried to the usual brown colour. It also hid old tree stumps which were very substantial but only two feet high. Now, an APC at speed tended to stop very suddenly when one of their tracks hit such a stump. Sadly, their young officers who rode with their heads sticking out of the turret on top, with their yellow scarf flying in the breeze, did not stop. After two had been taken to hospital with several teeth missing or with bruised jaws, their Colonel had called a halt to the morning exercise and called it a day. We were told to stay in camp and rest up.

Nifty came to me again with one of the men in tow:

"Dis 'ere is priva'e Kirkby." He stated. "'E's an engineer see, an' we cud build ya' a bridge across 'ha' nasty creek if you give us a day orf, Guv?"

"Done!" I replied. "Let's get this harbour more shipshape!" The men who were standing around though this analogy and my name was a good start to the day.

Nifty went back to the MI's store tent to scrounge tools and any other items of bridge-making equipment they might happen to have. Private/Engineer Kirkby headed off to the gulley to do his appraisal.

Nifty and a few helpers came back armed with a collection of saws, hammers. nails, ropes, shovels and picks. And a chainsaw. We had a whole platoon of willing volunteers and so the construction began.

Across the way, the curious Troopers heard a variety of load noises, including the sharp revving sound of a chainsaw cutting down some saplings.

"Keep it quiet!" I optimistically called to our lumber jacks in the hope that the neighbourhood colonel would be more concerned with his toothless troopers than the infantry about its nefarious business. I hoped that I would not have to fill in 'Lost and Damaged Reports" (in triplicate) for the few older saplings which were now coming down.

Private Kirkby was a good engineer and by that afternoon we had a cantilever bridge with a covering of compacted dirt and timber which could easily take a 4WD (and trailer) in any weather condition. I was very proud of my modern Legionnaires!

Nifty had also been at work and had raided the MI store yet again and with his very willing helpers. They had now provided a raised duckboard of paths throughout our camp, pallets beneath our tents to keep us all off the hard, and sometimes wet, ground and had even run a long extension cord and lamp across from the MI generator to provide us with electric light.

Finally, the troopers had recovered their toothless leaders and were ready to carry out their actions against the helpless infantry. Under orders to "retreat to a favourable spot for an attack", I took the platoon to a wooded creek crossing at the base of some very rugged country. Under normal conditions, I would have formed my defensive position well up into this rugged country where no track could tread. As a compromise to my 'enemy' status to help train the troopers and 'die like men', we settled on this creek crossing.

I was infantry-trained, so I could not give up all of the potential of such a site. I had mounted two of my machine guns so that they would fire down the creek towards the crossing, and the third was placed high up on the rocks with a good field of fire onto the crossing. I had also done the usual thing and planted small signs reading MINE in the creek crossing itself. The real army would not supply me with simulated mines which went off with a loud bang and give a nice cloud of purple smoke. The manual version would have to do. We took our positions, all camouflaged with the well-known cosmetic brand of brown and green.

After a very long wait (as usual) we heard the ominous sounds of tracked vehicles coming over the hill. One APC up and two back. Hatches closed and full of troopers.

The lead APC rumbled down and stopped just short of the creek crossing. These guys were no fools! The top hatch cover opened and a sergeant jumped down from his track. He ran forward, cupped his hands over his ears and began to trample all of my nice signs in the crossing into the dust. He turned to the assembled vehicles on the slopes.

"Mines cleared, Sir!" and ran back to his APC. The attacking vehicles swooped down into the creek crossing and went over unscathed.

"Bang, Bloody Bang!" said the exasperated Nifty lying in the greenery somewhere nearby.

We were soon surrounded by a large group of armed troopers who had surrounded my position and captured my guns. The cavalry had yet again won the day.

# Chapter Thirteen: Away all Boats!

Our ignoble defeat at the hands of the Mounted Infantry had been hailed as a great success in tactics for the Mounted Infantry and scrounging and engineering for Alpha Company. Their Colonel had contacted our Colonel and was full of praise. Shipley's Enemy Platoon had made its mark.

The idea of inter-unit cooperation had gone down well with the Colonel and Captain Willis was able to bask in our new-found glory, even though he contributed little. Flushed with success, our Colonel arranged for us to undergo an exercise with the C.M.F. Water Transport Squadron of the Corps of Engineers. This was to be a simulated attack on an enemy coastal village using the Water Transport's (WT) light landing craft. These were the flat-bottomed barges which had a drop-down ramp at their front and were called LCMs or Landing Craft Mechanized. Crewed by four water-borne Sappers each could hold a platoon of soldiers and other items as required.

Captain Burke had stayed in A-Company's lines one Tuesday night to explain the exercise that he and the Colonel had organised. We naturally assumed that he meant that it was the Colonel's plan and that Captain Burke had stood in the background offering strategic military opinions such as:

"Yes, Sir!"

"Good idea, Sir!"

"Three bags full, Sir!" and other expressions of support.

Meanwhile, back at A-Company, our new First Platoon which consisted of all of the Company's troops, Nifty and I and three trusted corporals were getting some valuable advice from WO2 Bauman who had been in landings in Korea as a young soldier and much later as an 'advisor' along the coast of Vietnam which no one knew about except the CIA.

This was to be a weekend exercise and was to be held in Broken Bay, a wide inlet and waterway north of the city and its populated harbour. As our regiment covered most of the northern part of the city with A-Company being right on the very northern outskirts, transportation to and from the regiment was not a problem. We would exercise during the day and retire to our respective depots overnight; the men to their Ordinary Ranks Club and the Sergeants and Officers to their combined Mess and salty dogs.

It was up to our gallant captain to carry out the intelligence and do a reconnaissance of our intended target. This was a National Fitness Camp for children sited on the shore abutting some very rugged and heavily-wooded hills on one arm of the bay. We would have a day's training on the Saturday doing improvised landings on a small beach further up the inlet. This was the only long strip of sand available and was in an area noted for its expensive water-side houses and wealthy inhabitants, many of whom were retired successful accountants.

On the Saturday, three LCM's had been provided by Water Transport and we were loaded off a ramp which was owned by the Royal North Bay Motor Boat Squadron who happened to have the Colonel of Water Transport as its Commodore. Everything going nicely! My platoon all marched onto out LCM and the other platoons from the regiment marched on to theirs.

Being 'full bottle' unlike the other platoons, thanks to WO2 Bauman, my troops face the rear of the LCM and crouched down, holding their rifles upper most; the gunners placed their three machine guns at the rear of each of the three section lines now in the well of the LCM. The ramp came down and we were off. WO2 Bauman had explained that the troops in the LCM should face backwards which gave them extra stability but also meant that their packs provided extra protection should small arms rounds pierce the front ramp. On hitting the beach, the men would turn, race out left, right and forward in three sections and form a semicircular perimeter prior to starting the attack. As the Platoon Commander, I was to lie up the ramp and call out the distances to the beach. Provided that no small arms rounds came through my part of the ramp, I would race out with my Sergeant and radio-operator and form the HQ group in the front and middle of the semicircle. Simple!

Away all boats! In we went for the first trial. Men all lined up and facing the rear. I lay on the ramp and called out the distances: 200 yards, 100 yards, 50 yards – it seemed rather weird doing an attack on well-healed suburbia where a curious crowd had gathered on the small pathway above the beach.

Bang! The ramp went down.

"Go! Go!" I shouted and lead my platoon out onto the beach.

"Jolly good show!" said some chinless and moustachioed wonder sitting on a deck chair above the beach and a few feet from my face. He raised his tall glass of Chardonnay in salute.

"Bravo!" came the shouts of the assembled multitude which had now gathered. D-Day was probably not like this! I couldn't imagine the Germans wandering down the beaches to greet the invading Allies with their glasses of Riesling or Hock!

We did this practise three times over that day, each time the assembled multitude had increased and their steadiness decreased in a direct proportion to the number of bottles of Chardonnay consumed. We retired dry and somewhat confused to salty dogs (Sergeants and Officers) and beer (OR's). The next day would be the real thing and before collapsing that night we all vowed that there would be no quarter on the enemy that we knew did not exist.

Our gallant Captain had done his intelligence, or so he told the Colonel of Water Transport who then informed us all next morning at the Royal North Bay

Motor Boat Squadron where he had spent the night. It was a tough life being a Colonel!

According to Captain Burke, the complex of the National Fitness Camp consisted of several long wooden buildings with playing field behind and going down to a long, narrow beach along the foreshore. The camp, he said was now unoccupied as most of the children should be on holidays. For all intents and purposes it could be regarded as any South East Asian fishing village. He, himself would act as coordinator and accompany the boats in. Luckily for us, he would be in LCM number three which would hit the beach first. The Colonel and his HQ staff would be waiting on the paved lookout on top of the high ridge at the rear of the camp where we would also meet our trucks. Our task was to attack the village and sweep through it (taking no prisoners!) and up the ridges to the lookout and car park on the heights.

Came the dawn. Away all boats! In we went. 200 yards. 100 yards, 50 yards. Ramp down Go! Go! Out onto the beach I ran with my platoon behind me. A perfect landing! A nice. Defensive semicircle laying on the wet sand ready for our gallant Captain to order us to sweep through the defenceless village (taking no prisoners!). It was then that the hidden enemy attacked!

Hoards of small children swarmed down from the huts and onto the beach to surround us like flies on a dustbin.

"Is that a real gun?" said some sleepy-eyed horror clutching his teddy bear.

"Go away, I hissed.

"Naft Orf!" growled Nifty at my elbow.

"Get your men off the beach!" shouted the Gnome who was now running up and down the beach falling over small groups of children.

The other hapless Platoon Commanders stood up and waved their hand to their platoons and echoed their Captains commands.

"1 Platoon will advance in line, HQ section leading" I yelled, standing up and thrusting my arm forward towards the nearest pathway between the huts. "In single file. Move!"

With a considerable number of "excuse mes" I led my platoon off the beach and down the long pathway which led to the playing fields and the ridges beyond. Bedraggled teachers and National Fitness Instructors wandered out of their dormitories to see what had disturbed their usually peaceful Sunday morning.

We climbed over the small fence at the far side of the playing fields and went into the heavily wooded area at the foot of a rather steep ridge. I had read the exercise map, something which had escaped the gullibility of the other Platoon Commanders. Straight up! Bearing 270 degrees magnetic. I was thankful that I always carried my compass.

Up we went. Through the thick scrub with occasional grunts and oaths as men fell over logs and got tangled in the briers. Finally, we burst onto the bitumen road which led to the wide car park where the Colonel in his car and our trucks were waiting. I had overshot my bearing and so had to walk back a little way to the end of the lookout. I told the men to fall out and have a breather by the side of the road. Nifty somehow produced a large bag of sweets from his pack and was now passing them around.

"Where are the others? asked the Colonel, waddling up to where I was standing.

"Behind me. Sir." Was all I could say, not having a clue where they were.

At that moment, Captain Burke burst belligerently through the bushes to our left and stumbled over the gutter of the car park, losing his cap in the process.

"Where are the others, Mr Shipley?" asked the ruffled Captain, pully some twigs out of his uniform then jumping to attention and saluting when he saw the Colonel.

"Behind me, Sir… somewhere." Was all I could say.

The Colonel and the Captain wandered back to the edge of the carpark to look for their missing platoons. Nothing but the quiet blue of the bay in the distance with the morning sunlight shimmering on the water.

From somewhere below came a faint "hello"!

Nifty looked at me and raised an eyebrow. "What a farce!" he said conspiratorially.

Another faint "hello" came from further down the ridges, but this time it was even fainter.

Two hours later, Captain Burke, by now a complete mental wreck having been rebuked several times by the Colonel about his intelligence (or lack of it) and knowing that his chances of soon becoming a Major had evaporated, stumble up to us and said; "Lieutenant Shipley. Take two of your men and go and find the other platoons."

I volunteered two of my Platoon who had proven to be good bushman and plunged back into the scrub.

A series of shouts and considerable thrashing about in the scrub finally led to the discovery of one of the platoons who had sat down to await their fate whilst their officer wandered about nearby looking for a trail which did not exist. I pointed him back along my way with the instruction to keep going uphill in that direction. The other platoon was more difficult to find until we had arrived back at the playing field fence. Unsure of which way to go, they had retreated downhill back to the National Fitness Camp where they also had camped on the edge of the playing field. I knew my bearings from this starting point so led them back up into the bush and to the car park above.

Our amphibious attack on the enemy fishing village had been a stupendous failure. D-Day had never been like this!

# Chapter Fourteen: A New Hope

Everyone had decided to keep a low profile after our aqueous adventures. The Colonel was never invited back to share Chardonnay with his WT friend at the Royal North Bay Motor Boat Squadron, Captain Willis resolved never to go near the water again and my brother officers at HQ were sent off to do a navigation course. The Gnome now spent most of his Tuesday nights behind his own desk at A-Company making everyone's life miserable. Everyone, that is except WO2 Bauman who seemed to have a permanent smile on his dial at the thought of his Officer Commanding being pursued by a vicious enemy hoard of seven-year-olds. There was always a way to get rid of an unpleasant officer.

I had been promoted to First Lieutenant not long afterwards, but the training at our little outpost had degenerated into 'in house' lectures, drill, more lectures and more drill. This went on for months. The Gnome annoyed Jimmy O'Halloran by confiscating his collection of training manuals and spent much of his time finding the most boring sections of military monotony available. 'Water Resupply in the Field' was one of the first topics which the good Captain (or Gnome) had decided that the officers and men should rediscover. Moreover, he had discovered the potential of the overhead projector and so had it moved into the drill hall so that all and sundry could listen to his discourse on that topic.

Death by boredom was not a new tactic in the C.M.F. The men often had their intellect decreased by such lectures at camp, but usually it was given by some sergeant who had some understanding of how soldiers' brains worked and would often slip a 'motivational image' onto the OHP or in the slide sequence to wake up any 'dozy digger' whose head had dropped down from the 'sitting easy' position. This usually came in the form of some pneumatic-looking girl in a swimsuit reinforcing the topic of the lecture. In this case, it would not have been hard to insert some bikini-clad river nymph into a harangue about water resupply. Not so with the Gnome. It was doubtful that such concepts as 'motivational image' or any other teaching style other than 'the harangue' had ever entered his mind. Even having an audio-visual aid was a compromise. He had to go.

The chance for WO2 Bauman to exert some of his guerrilla tactics using his extensive spy network came a few months later. Apart from having the ability, like all Warrant Officers, to suddenly appear from nowhere, WO2 Bauman also knew exactly what was going on at all times, even if he pretended to be the older, pre-retirement member of the Regular Army Cadre of the regiment. It came about in a most unexpected manner.

One Tuesday night, he wondered past the training office where I was sitting attempting to prepare a theoretical lesson on Counter Ambush Drill from the appropriate grey manual which had been dispensed to me by the Gnome earlier that evening.

"Give the men a lesson on Counter Ambush Drill, Mr Shipley." He had ordered. "You may use my OHP if you must." This was a rare moment of generosity from the Gnome.

"What are you preparing, Mr. Shipley?" WO2 Bauman asked benignly. Of course, he knew exactly what I was doing.

"Counter Ambush Drill, Sergeant Major." I innocently replied. WO2 Bauman looked at the manual and shook his head.

"A load of rubbish in that" he said, stabbing at the manual with a hardened, bony finger. "If you are silly enough to get caught in a VC[8] ambush then the only 'counter' you can do is die quietly!" he grumped.

He then sat down and gave me an impromptu lesson on ambush tactics. The manual had advocated several steps that a luckless platoon would use to overpower someone stupid enough to ambush them. This required:

1. going to ground and returning fire directly in the enemy who would be hiding in the hedgerows to one side of the road;
2. sending the back two sections back down the road who would then move quietly through the hedgerows (using the village steeple for a bearing); and
3. having these two sections form up in line abreast and move down upon the unsuspecting enemy from their side of the hedgerow.

---

[8] Viet Cong – the communist guerrillas in Vietnam

If this was not an option, then turning left or right and barging through said hedgerows with bayonets fixed and much firepower was the only other option.

"No hedgerows nor village steeples in the jungles of SE Asia" he said "so you're stuffed! In a likely ambush site, we would have every second man hold a grenade with the pin held by his thumb. If we were ambushed, they would throw left and right and then we would all bug out ASAP back the way we came."

That method sounded rather extreme and there were no OHP slides that I could prepare to do such a tactic justice.

WO2 Bauman then enlightened me on the usual VC method of ambush which I thought more practical than a few shots from behind a hedgerow. Their method involved a V-shaped formation with the open end facing down the point of entry of the luckless ambushees. Fire would therefore be interlaced from both sides and our Counter Ambush Drill would be fairly useless. Charging off into the jungle (or hedgerows) would mean falling into a punji pit, a deep pit full of spiked sticks and not conducive to the good health of the patrol.

"Not a good topic for a theoretical lecture." He said, walking off with a knowing smile.

Faced with the dilemma of teaching something about ambushes I went to a superior source of help; my Sergeant, Nifty Nev.

"No probs, Guv!" he responded to my plea for help. "Ya lec'ure's on nex' week did ya' say? Well I jus appen 'o knah 'ha the gud Cap'ain is goin' up 'o the big Guv nex' week an so we can 'ave a righ' gud shah 'ere." He gave me a 'wink, wink, nod, nod, say no more' look and disappeared.

He returns a short time later.

"Righ',we 'ave all 'he necessities faw a gud field lesson 'ere, Guv! Nah I jus' 'appen 'o knah 'ha' up the frog and toad apiece an' in 'he Na'ional Park 'here's an old overgrown army 'raining ground. Tracks, bunkers, 'he lo'! You wi'h me?"

I didn't but it sounded interesting and far better than another OHP lecture. He went on.

"Nah, I jus' also 'appen 'o knah where 'here's some old boxes ov blank ammunition an' a few nice li"le red flares, like. They should do 'he job!"

The scenario being outlined was both frightening and interesting. A quick vision of my battered Army Law Manual flashed for an incredibly brief moment:

*'It is both an offence civil and military for a military unit during peacetime to hold within the confines of their premises ammunition and pyrotechnics of any type including blank ammunition, red flares etc etc…'*

"That's against regulations!" I squeaked.

"No probs Guv!" came the reply. "'ha' place is so cuv'd wi'h bush that no one will knah 'ha' we 'ave even bin 'here. An' I' will good 'raining faw 'he lads. Tha' Bauman wontt 'ave a mind, even ith 'e did find arh! Leaf it to me." With that he scurried out of the Training Room to put his nefarious plans into operation.

With some trepidation, I prepared two lessons: one with appropriate overhead projections (no motivational image) and in triplicate as usual; and the other on paper which could easily be destroyed of a small-scale outdoor exercise involving the Company's bored soldiers – other officers and NCO's excluded. Nothing going on at the moment and the good Captain still at his desk, I grabbed Nifty and went on a short reconnaissance 'up the road apiece'. It was a great place for a night exercise, with a main track winding downhill past some old and now overgrown concrete bunkers.

I would have a small group of my most trusted men, including Nifty set up flares attached to tripwires across the main track and then forming into a small V down track to be the ambushing unit. They would each have a few rounds of blank ammunition provided by Nifty.

When complete, I took my decoy lesson (OC's copy) to the OC (Gnome) and handed it to him. He seemed satisfied that at least one of his officers was still awake and perused its contents.

"What's this need for the men to be in full combat gear, Mr Shipley?" he asked with the usual frown. How someone could talk and frown at the same time was one of the Gnomes most interesting talents.

"Realism, Sir" I said with enthusiasm "We can 'play act' the drill when I finish the talk, Sir." I lied.

"Yes…umm..humph..yes! That sounds like a good idea. Part of your training at SCOTU huh?"

"Yes, Sir. Regular Army MIT course, Sir." That made a good impression.

"Umm..humph..well, I'm sorry now that I won't be there to see it next week. Conference with the Colonel, you know." He confided.

"I'm sorry, too, Sir!" I lied even more strongly.

Tuesday night came and the troops, now in full combat gear were ushered into the drill hall looking quite bewildered; the OHP and chairs being set up for yet another exercise. The other officers and Sergeants had been 'squared away' by Nifty, whatever that meant but I was not going to ask. WO2 Bauman sat quietly at his desk going through some paperwork for the second time.

Having ensured that the Gnome had indeed driven off to HQ, I gave Nifty the nod to get his ambushers off to their 'killing ground'. I took charge of the bewildered group, formed them up into three ranks, left turn and off we marched out of the depot, keeping to the side of the highway which ran north out of the city's outskirts.

At the start of the heavily-wooded National Park (entry permits required), I sat the men down in a small clearing just off the road and commenced my lesion on Counter Ambush drill as amended by WO2 Bauman.

My motivation step here had been the need for full combat gear and the retreat from the dreaded OHP in the drill hall. The men were now very much awake and wondering what this crazy officer and his even crazier sergeant was about to do next. Having gone through the objectives of the lesson:

"By the end of this lesson you will all know

1.  how it feels to be in a modern ambush;
2.  be without hedgerows when you need them; and
3.  simulate dying like men."

They understood the next lesson step which was the rationale for doing the lesson, that is; why it was necessary not to get into an ambush in the first place.

Warning them of the fact that it was night and that there was an active enemy and that they were in for a nasty surprise, I sent the lead section down the track. Within a very short space of time, their forward scout, ever vigilant tripped over the planted trip wire. With a small, muffled 'pop' the red flare went off. It had been expertly attached high up in a tree just down the track. From both sides came the loud, high-pitched 'pops' of SLRs firing blank rounds in the air.

"S**t!" said the forward scout. Some of the 'old timers' went to ground in a defensive position whilst the 'new boys' just stood in befuddlement, rubbing their eyes.

"Right!" I called. "War's over! Come onto the track!" I called. Nifty and his men came smiling onto the track. Their part in the exercise being a great piece of fun. I sat the troops who were still standing down and continued my lesson about being in an ambush and how dashing through hedgerows and falling into pits was not a great idea.

The lesson had been a great success! The men all laughed at how each other had been scared witless when the flare went off. The 'older hands', a couple of whom had returned from Vietnam nodded their approval and gave their mates a quick wink. We walked easy in file back to the depot and our respective messes to talk about the night's training.

The next Tuesday night, the Gnome called me into his office.

"What's going on. Mr. Shipley? I've just had a complaint from one of the local civilian population about gunshots going off here last night! What!

What!" he cried making small jumping movements like a demented toad in his chair.

"Shots, Sir?" I innocently asked. "We are not allowed to fire shots, Sir. We're the army!" I protested.

"Shots! Shot! Mr Shipley!" he continued going even darker in the face.

"Fettlers, Sir." Came a voice from behind my left shoulder. WO2 Bauman had suddenly appeared from nowhere as was his habit.

"Fettlers? Fettlers?" The Gnome echoed.

"Yes, Captain Willis" came the soft tones of the Sergeant Major. "Railway workers are called fettlers." He responded like a wise old schoolteacher assisting a dull child.

"I know what a fettler, CSM is," the exasperated Gnome replied. "What has it to do with gunshots?"

"Well, Sir," the old schoolmaster continued, "they often work at night because of the reduced rail traffic and will put detonators onto the tracks to warn them of approaching trains. That's probably what the civilian heard." WO2 Bauman also had a great talent in telling great tales whilst keeping a military straight face.

The Gnome thought about this. And thought again. Finally, his eyes assumed the dull, almost prone position and his lips quavered at their edges.

"Yes…perhaps you may be right," he replied, the eyelids once again being raised to full mast and the quivering lips went to a smile of understanding… Wrong in this case.

"Yes…Fettlers, of course. That's it!" and reached for his telephone to pass on his new-found wisdom to the complainant. WO2 Bauman gave me a wink and disappeared equally as fast as his first appearance. I turned quickly and retreated.

The next week, an inspection team from our main HQ showed up. Under the command of one of the new and upwardly-mobile young captains from HQ staff, the team of experienced NCO's passed by the Gnome, who had no idea as to what was going on, and went straight to the hidden supplies of blank ammunition and red flares which were hidden in the obvious place, our usually empty Armory. WO2 Bauman had struck!

Our gallant Captain was 'invited' back to the main HQ for a conference with the Colonel to explain these nasty little surprises. It was 'not the done thing' for a C.M.F. unit to have ammunition. A-Company went into a collective fit of laughter after they had departed. WO2 Bauman just sat at his desk with a satisfied grin on his face. Nifty just looked at the open door of the Armory and plotted where he would hide the next batch of 'jack' ammo he would obtain from his network.

It was a matter of good luck and convenience that my university timetable changed a few weeks later at the start of a new term and I was unable to parade on a Tuesday night. I gave my apologies to our new Acting Officer Commanding, the new and upwardly-mobile captain who had now acquired his own company and requested that I be attached to some other unit to meet my yearly commitment. WO2 Bauman again came to my aid and suggested that he had heard that SCOTU, of which I was a graduate, needed some new additional officers for their mid-year camp. The appropriate papers just happened to be in his hand at the time and they were completed (in triplicate) my me with the speed of a moving bullet.

Two weeks later, and in full uniform I drove though the gates of the Regular Army's base west of the city. This was something new! SCOTU had moved from the old Victoria Barracks and the dreaded Stalag Bandicoot to new quarters in the Regular Army's base. There was hope for the C.M.F. yet!

I reported to their new HQ and their equally new Commanding Officer, Colonel Dagworthy. He gave me a quick, disinterested welcome and explained that. As a 'supernumerary' I would be quartered in the now-vacant Regular Army lines and take my meals in their Officers Mess. Things were now really looking up. My duties would be to supplement his officers training routine with some drill, academic lectures and a range day with live firing. This sounded well enough, so I about faced and went off to find my new 'diggings'.

Into a nice, clean brick accommodation block, I walked down the carpeted corridor until I passed an open door.

"Welcome to 'the Motel' came a pleasant voice from inside. "You must be Shipley?" it continued.

I went in and saw another first lieutenant sitting on one of the two comfortable-looking beds. He stood up and extended his hand which I took after throwing my kitbag and gear onto the other bed.

"Mears, the name!" he said and sat back down on his bed. "It's good to be back with the old unit" he continued, "but things have changed!"

David Mears was also a former graduate of SCOTU as a member of Number 20 Course and had been posted to an armoured unit so he wore a yellow lanyard on his battle dress. He went on to describe the changes he had discovered from their RSM, WO2 Chris McCrery. My old instructor Sergeant McCrery had become more scary! Lieutenant - Colonel Jaeger had been promoted and now wore the red tabs of a full colonel and was even now trying to shake some sense into the senior staff at Sydney Command. Most of the other NCOs had retired and the younger officers returned to their units. The new SCOTU was greatly diminished and was under its usual entitlement for Officers/Instructors. Hence our attachment.

Apart from decamping to more professional surroundings, Mears said with a degree of laconic cynicism that we were now also training female officers. He made this comment to see if I would bite.

No luck! I had had some little experience with my failed action against another unit of the armoured corps which also had a few female soldiers in their ranks. I had found them to be extremely efficient, both diligent and precise in their duties. A little scary when compared to some of the slacko's in A-Company! And they were also smart enough to keep their heads away from turret hatches when travelling through long grass.

Mears and I were going to enjoy this camp. We had excellent accommodation which could easily have been in any motel in Civvy Street we also had the run of the Regular Officers' Mess. This almost empty for the time being, the Regs being on some major exercise up north. Our only other companions for meals and at night were a group of very senior officers here for a short conference on national defence strategy. Full colonel was the lowest rank in this prestigious group, but they made us comfortable when we two lowly subalterns wandered into their company for lunch.

No 'cold-meat salad here! And certainly, no white bread and lemon spread! Our food was obtained from a glass-topped servery which contained a bewildering array of both hot and cold food items served by the army's professional caterers. No ex-army cooks recruited from the streets of the city! Mears also mentioned, sotto voice so the rest of the C.M.F. would not overhear, that we also had a batman. Great surprise! It would be a new highlight in my military life of some eight years to have someone else to press my uniform and blacken my boots GP. I was not too sure of how this would work as I was so used to doing my own thing that having a personal army-style butler was going to be a strange undertaking.

Mears had already had an in-depth interview with SCOTU Colonel Dagworthy – well it lasted a few more brief minutes more than my short time – and had a written schedule of our training duties. My first encounter would be at 0800 tomorrow when I would give the courses their first drill lesson on how to wheel about. Easy for an infantry officer but Mear's armoured corps had tracked vehicles, he joked so he knew nothing about wheels.

After a sumptuous roast beef dinner with wine, Mears and I had a free night and so wondered into the bar area. Here an assortment of Full Colonels, some of them getting fuller, Brigadiers and the odd General (probably!) were standing about or sitting about at one of the many oaken tables.

"Come on in, gentlemen!" the odd General called cheerfully. Mears and I wandered over into the group like two schoolboys being invited to a teachers' party. Whilst there was a good three-rank difference in our status, we were made to feel like part of the mess (well…almost).

We decided to purchase our own drinks as the seniors had started out early in to most expensive bottles of Chardonnay which had been especially indented for by the Mess Committee before their arrival. Even our combined first lieutenant salaries could survive a return shout of Chardonnay.

Soon the dice came out at the bar and the seniors had decided to play Liar Dice which was like a bluffing game of poker with five dice rather than cards. Their memories of their subaltern days long forgotten, they encouraged us to join, assuming that mere first lieutenants had no knowledge of the game. Luckily for us, both Mears and I had come up through the ranks and were well experienced with the concept of bluff. A few quick games in which we won and had

Chardonnay thrust upon us, convinced the seniors that they were not going to have some fun at our expense. Mears and I gratefully retired, excusing ourselves because of an early training schedule the next day; the seniors not having to rise before their 1000 hours conference.

The next day, having almost recovered from the Chardonnay exercise the night before, I dressed in my now pressed combat greens, black belt and boots GP and Hats KF and went out looking for my drill students; Mears had an easy afternoon prior to a lecture in the afternoon about the tactics of the Armoured Corp. I was soon accosted by two, very smart Regular Sergeants of Infantry.

"Morning, Sir!" said the smartest giving me a very crisp salute. "I'm Sergeant Blake and this is Sergeant Noakes.  We have been attached to you to assist in your training."

Dumfounded, I showed them my training schedule for the day which was largely drill.

"No problems, Sir!" said Blake." Leave it to us!" Turning to his companion he continued "Left and Right Wheel, Noaksey! Just up our alley!" and off they went, leaving me with a clipboard to wander around looking important and for someone to give me a salute. Something I had vowed never to do. Morning Tea in the Officer's Mess was still a long two hours away.

This seemed to be a regular pattern and Mears and I soon fell into it and both polished up our clipboards for each daily exercise of wandering about between meals. Actually, it was not all just hard work. Occasionally, the two sergeants needed an officer present, such as on the range where we watched the keen cadets fire a variety of weapons under the watchful tutelage of Sergeants Blake and Noakes. We were both relived to find that the OMC which had the potential to fall apart and spray bullets everywhere but at the target, had been replaced by the latest F1 submachine gun. Grenade practice had also been removed from the syllabus as had bayonet fighting which had usually been carried out by soldiers stripped to the waist destroying bags of chaff hung from frames. The graphic descriptions of what would be the real-life consequences of such actions cause cadets such as my old friend Dozy Donaldson to faint. Having female cadets doing bayonet fighting was beyond imagination.

The highlight of our usefulness at SCOTU mid-year camp came one night when a lecture from 2000 hours to 2100 hours was to be given on my old nemesis, 'Water Resupply in the Field'. As the infantry member of the 'supernumerary' team, it was to be my lecture, but Mears kindly suggested that as it was a very important topic, he would help. Consequently, whilst the Sergeants Blake and Noakes drilled our students hard that afternoon, Mears and I prepared the lesson 'par excellence' on this, the most boring of military topics.

Everything prepared, our students were marched in at 2000, (as an officer I had learnt that meant 8 pm) by Sergeant Blake.

"Left! Right! Left! Right! Sit! Remove your hats. Sit easy!" came the familiar refrain. After a very hard days work with much physical activity flowed by a decent meal, the last thing that the tired Cadets needed was a boring lecture on how to get water. A big motivation step was needed here. And Mears and I had a spectacular event planned.

The Cadets looked up through sleepy eyes as the curtain of the small stage opened slowly. Mears was sitting at a small table in the centre of the stage. He was dressed in full blues uniform, which in the Armour Corp was covered with considerable amounts of shiny brass and yellow stripes. His black beret with its rather showy Cavalry badge sat on the table and he had a class half filled with whiskey in his hand thanks to a quick trip to the Officers' Mess.

The Cadets now looked up with more curiosity.

Mears started into the reason why it was so important to have water. He raised his glass to demonstrate then did a 'double take' when he realised that his 'whiskey and water' was sans water.

"Damn!" he muttered and turned to the wings of the stage. "Steward! Steward! Where's my damn water?

Suddenly from Stage Right, I entered dressed in the white uniform of a steward (thanks also to the Officers' Mess staff). I marched with good solid strides, of which even a Reg Drill Instructor would have been proud. Bang! I came to a sudden halt at Mear's table and banged my right boot down heavily and gave a Guards-style salute.

"Sah!" I shouted.

"Where's my bally water, you dozy steward?" the 'aggravated' Cavalry Officer yelled.

"Sah!" came the responding yell, another crisp Guards-style salute. A smart about face and I marched off.

Mears continued his quiet discourse about why water in the field was most important.

From the Right wing I marched loudly, holding a full jug of water in my left hand. Left! Right! Left! Right! Bank! Right foot to the floor, Right arm up for another Guards-style salute.

"Damn it all, man. Pour my water!" Mears said, glaring up at his stupid steward. He turned and faced his now very attentive audience who were now wide awake seeing such an exaggerated pantomime from their officers.

Mears continued explaining the need for water and the objectives of this lecture. I continued pouring the water – under orders to do just that. The water was poured. It rose quickly top the top of the glass. It flowed over top of the glass and onto the desk. Some of the audience started to giggle. The water flowed across the desk and onto the stage. The steward, head high and eyes straight ahead in good military order continued pouring.

Mears having finished the objectives of the lecture, now became the 'aggravated officer' again and jumped to his feet, yelled some Armoured Corps oath and chased me of the stage; stage right. The curtain closed.

It soon opened and I stood there, having wheeled the omnipresent OHP across our small lake into the centre of the stage. Applause from our appreciative audience who now looked forward to my lecture, interspersed with some anecdotes from my own bad experience connected to water supply in the field.

At the end of the camp, Colonel Dagworthy gave us a very short 'thank you' and dismissed us both. Mears to return to his cavalry unit and me to an uncertain future in my unit now that I could not parade on Tuesday nights. I could not really become a detached officer all of my career and I did not feel like transferring to units which paraded on other nights.

I took stock of my situation once at home and realised that the university was probably going to play nightly roulette with my program of studies,

which were now also getting more intense. I made
the very reluctant decision to resign my commission
and leave the C.M.F. for good.

I had not won my personal war with the
reactionaries of C.M.F High Command but there
were glimpses of hope that others would win it for
me: Colonel Jaeger was already making waves at
High Command; units were now accepting excellent
female officers and well as other ranks and there
appeared to more support from and integration with
the Regular Army. There was even a rumour that
one day, the C.M.F. may evolve into a fully
integrated Army Reserve and play a more
professional and well-equipped role in the nation's
defence.

# About the Author

**2Lt P.T. Scott, circa 1973**

Dr. Peter Terence Scott was born in Sydney, Australia and had a professional teaching career spanning over forty years; eight of these as a member of the Citizens' Military Forces or C.M.F. which later evolved into the Army Reserve. In some regards, his military career contained many of the events given in this book. Like Tom Shipley, he started his career as a Private soldier, having volunteered after being deferred from National Service. Later, he attended the Officer Cadet Training Unit and was Commissioned into the Infantry as a Second Lieutenant. During his military career, he also studied at university part time and obtained a Bachelor of Science degree and later Masters' Degrees in Science and Educational Administration and a Doctorate in Education. In 1988, he joined the Australian Naval Cadets and wore a Naval Lieutenant's uniform for twelve years. Trained in 'Tall Ships', he was Commanding Officer of Training Ship *Magnus*, Australian Naval Cadets.

# Other Books by the Author

### FICTION

**Letters from San Rafael** (as Hernan Moreno Ruiz). Set in South America in the 1880's, this is a collection of letters smuggled home by Don Hernan Moreno, an Intelligence officer of the Peruvian Army who has been captured by the Ecuadorans during a border dispute. Taken to the fortified hacienda in Banos, in the mountains of Ecudor, he and his sargeant, Garcia, are treated as honoured guests. Each of the ten stories tells of the life and times of people in the hacienda and beyond. The final chapter is the climax of the entire book.

**The Ice Ship.** Set mainly in the Antarctic in the 1840's, this is the story of the survival of the crew of the futuristic auxiliary steam whaler, the AUSTRALIS which has become trapped in the ice following its voyage south along the Antarctic Peninsula. Based upon actual observations and experience of the author during a 2011 voyage into the same region on a small ex-research vessel.

**The Innocence of Tom Shipley.** Is the first novel about young teacher Tom Shipley. It begins during his days at High School and his penchant as a Laboratory Prefect in making explosives and other prankish devices, follows him through similar acts at Teachers College and then out into his first appointment at age nineteen into the profession of teaching. At a brand-new school in Canberra, he finds that as the sole Science teacher, he is now the Acting Head of Department charged with establishing this subject at the school and equipping and managing several laboratories and new incoming staff.

## NON-FICTION

**Adventures in Earth Science** is an in-depth, traditional Earth Science textbook on Geology, Meteorology, Oceanography and Astronomy. The latest scientific information has been given in the text including chapters on climate change and the future use of fuels and energy. The book contains over 700 pages, 1200 photographs and illustrations mostly taken by the author. It also includes 32 video links taken by the author to explain various skills as well as excursions to many exotic places in support of the text. Also has companion **Teachers' Guide** and **Laboratory Manual**.

The contents of this book have also been rearranged into the **Adventures in Earth Science Series** of eight smaller individual books in both electronic and A5 print editions.

Exploration Science

Fossils- Life in the  Rocks

Riches from the Earth

A Dangerous Planet: Volcanoes and Earthquakes

Rocks - Building The Earth

Changing the Surface: Weathering And Erosion

Through Sea and Sky: Oceanography and Meteorology

Beyond Planet Earth: Astronomy

**Adventures in Earth and Environmental Science** is a two-volume textbook on the environment, how it is monitored and implications for the future. They come in electronic format and as A4-sized print editions with a **Laboratory Manual** for each volume and a **Teachers' Guide**.

**Surviving Global Warming - A Guide for the Future** is a comprehensive explanation of the natural and man-made causes of global warming with data from a wide range of reputable scientific bodies such as CSIRO and NASA. Written with many innovative suggestions for coping with the consequences of future global warming at the home, local and government levels. It comes as an electronic or printed edition.

A concise reference book on going into the wild places of the Earth based on the author's extensive experience as a hiker, caver, geologist, Infantry Officer, ski instructor and leader of several youth groups. Topics include basic equipment, food, water, shelter, rope work, navigation and communications. The book is designed to be carried in pocket or backpack to where mobile phone signals may be lost. It is available in Kindle format as well as paperback and it is recommended that mobile phone users install it as a stand-alone document.

All of these books are available in electronic format for any PC or tablet in Kindle format which can be read on any device using the free Kindle App. Or as print editions. Available at all Internet book outlets or from **Felix Publishing** by contacting them at:

info.felixpublishing@gmail.com

www.ingramcontent.com/pod-product-compliance
Lightning Source LLC
Chambersburg PA
CBHW070621170726
48291CB00003B/826